I0594535

I wish to acknowledge the Turrbal and Yuggera Peoples, the custodians of the lands I wrote this book, work and live on. I pay my respect to Elders past and present, and acknowledge the rich and ongoing culture of storytelling of Aboriginal and Torres Strait Islander peoples.

OUR DREAMS WERE WAKING UP

SCOTTY MCDONALD

NATIONAL
LIBRARY
OF AUSTRALIA

A catalogue record for this
book is available from the
National Library of Australia

NOVEMBER 2022

1

"Do property managers need to tell you you'll see people kill themselves when you sit on your balcony?" I texted Andy.

"No. Get off your balcony and meet someone, get a drink somewhere." His reply was quick but sharp. He was clearly on a date. "No one has success on Tinder like real estate agents," he tells me at the end of almost every weekend.

I sat there slowly sipping the latest addition to my brewery's tap, an apple cider, condensation pooling down its sides in the warm night air. Someone had been peering over the edge of the Story Bridge into the water of the Brisbane River for too long and was now pacing back and forth. I'd seen this before.

When I moved into the apartment nearly two years earlier, I'd bragged about my view of the river, the bridge, the amazing New Year fireworks and how great it was just sitting out on my balcony while day crossed into night and the skyscraper jungle around me went from bustling, busy office workers, to people out for dinner with old friends, colleagues catching up over beers and cleaners getting to work on preparing the place for tomorrow.

I wasn't prepared for what happened on the bridge, though.

At least once every month I'd seen someone attempt to take their life jumping from the tall steel structure. The first time I was trying to work out what they were up to, when suddenly they jumped. I was so shocked I stood there frozen, realising only as the ambulance and police sped into the park next to the river that I probably should have called 000 as soon as it happened.

The second time I saw someone "making plans," I was prepared. I called the police. It was a busy Saturday night. The person on the other end of the line made it clear that I didn't have any reason to be disturbing someone just "hanging out on the bridge". By the time they sent a car out she'd decided to live another day and I spent the night annoyed the police hadn't taken me seriously.

Then I felt responsible. If I couldn't even get the police to take this seriously, then who else was going to be there for people during such a lonely experience?

I lost someone I cared about when I was a teenager. She died in a terrifying moment, all alone. I don't think it's possible to ever fully recover from that. I'd spent years speaking to a counsellor about it, but when all was said and done, I was still burning hot with anger in a deep part of my heart that I knew could never forgive the people responsible.

I wasn't ready to talk about it, but keeping watch over the bridge had become an obsession. It had started with me eating dinner on the balcony every night; then sticking around for a few drinks after dinner; then realising I avoided going out at night because I felt comfort in being there, waiting to help in someone's most terrible time.

I knew it was silly and useless and that eventually I'd need to talk to someone about it, but there was some place inside me hoping to take back that moment I wasn't there for her.

I walked into my kitchen and grabbed my binoculars to get a better look.

That face, I recognised that face instantly. Wearing the hurt and despair, feeling at the end of their rope. I froze in my spot.

I didn't want to go down there; I didn't want to have that conversation. I had always wondered how it would go if I knew the person on the bridge, but this seemed way too difficult.

I didn't have a choice, though. I couldn't be in the position where I had a choice to be with someone in their worst moment, but I'd decided it was too hard.

I spent five minutes semi-preparing to go down, finding thongs for my feet, then shoes, brushing my teeth, checking I looked decent for outside - as if anyone was going to notice. I went back to the balcony.

Still there. Still looking over the edge.

"Okay," I said to myself, "Let's do this."

MAY 2012

2

As soon as I decided to pick up three Scotch Finger biscuits and a chocolate-covered bear, I regretted it. Andy had returned to Dan and me with his family friend Cal and her two friends much quicker than expected. He was clearly in love with Cal, but of course he'd never admit it. Now instead of being weird, loud and a bit uncoordinated, I was all those things plus had no manners because I took more than my fair share of biscuits at social functions.

"Uh, guys, this is Cal," Andy told us while awkwardly motioning toward his friend, who we'd seen a stack of photos of but never actually met. She was shorter than I expected.

"This is Dan and Josh," he continued, now moving his awkward motion toward us.

Dan was leaning against the fence of the Cavendish College Girls School pool, holding a level of cool that I was so envious of him for. As we stood in our sister school's courtyard, surrounded by small clusters of hormone-filled flirty grade II's from Camp Hill's two single-sex schools, I felt like the most awkward person in the group by far. My grey school trousers felt way too high, I'm sure my tie made me look like a little boy dressing up as the Prime Minister or something, and I had no idea what to do with these biscuits conspicuously filling up my hands.

I looked to Dan for comfort, but his body language could not have been more comfortable. For someone whose only female friend was his cousin, he was way too chilled out in this environment.

Cal responded brightly, but her eyes kept darting to her two friends by her side.

"Hi, um, this is Lauren and Amber!" she pointed to each of her friends, and we reached out and shook hands.

The three girls were giggly, but they seemed mature - like they thought about things years beyond where we were at. They certainly appeared more at ease than I felt.

"I don't usually take fist fulls of... Arnott's family share pack biscuits" I said, while obviously reading the name off the packet on the table next to us.

"Yea, I was pretty worried you hadn't eaten for like a week or something," Amber replied, then giggled along with her friends.

"I'm just saying, Scotch Fingers are the god-tier of afternoon snack foods," I presented one of the biscuits to the group, jokingly in awe of the snack.

"Anyone want a Finger" I asked, before immediately realising what I'd said, "Not like that..." I continued as the group burst out into laughter - the ice had been broken, and I was trying really hard not to blush.

"Settle down buddy, has it really been that long since you last spoke to a female?" Dan mockingly patted my back.

"I have no idea what these children are laughing at" Amber said trying to compose herself, "I'll take one" she continued with a smile that said she knew she'd saved me from embarrassment, and light blue eyes flashing me a look that seemed to say "that was fun, let's play again some time."

I snapped off a Finger and gave it to her.

She was blonde, which was annoying because since grade 4 I'd decided I only liked brunette girls. Blonde girls seemed too unreal, too model like, maybe too unattainable for me.

"Wow, god-tier might have been under selling it," she mocked after her first bite, "to think the grade 11 social afternoon tea between the Cavendish College ladies and First Grammar gentlemen would bring such delicacy," she continued in a fake British accent.

A weird feeling hit me, like I'd instantly developed a crush on her, or more like something in my brain said, "this is the kind of girl you should have a crush on," and so I did. Out of nowhere my stomach filled with butterflies. Unexpected insecurity washed over me and I felt like I was competing against boys I didn't know existed in a race I knew nothing about.

3

THE FRIDAY after Amber and I met, we stayed up the entire night chatting on messenger, telling each other the stories of our lives, our favourite foods, places, people, movies.

I was convinced that she must be the kind of girl that has a great group of male friends. I couldn't work out if staying up all night chatting was a special, only us thing, or if in a week or two I'd be struggling to get her attention. While I had her attention, I was giving her as many reasons as possible to want to keep chatting with me.

Then it happened. At 3:26am, multiple emergency sirens pierced through the dark, cold and eerily still May morning outside my window, as first responders raced down the main road nearby.

Josh: Holy Moly, someone's in trouble!

Amber: Oh no! Why's that?

Josh: I reckon at least 3 ambulances just sped by my place. That stuff always freaks me out - especially at night.

Amber: Wait! I just heard them too! Like I can still hear them in the distance.

Josh: Haha, what? Where do you live?

Amber: In Camp Hill, like behind the all-night supermarket.

Josh: Seriously! I live on Wattle St! Like literally one block back from the shops.

Amber: No way! I'm on Bottlebrush St!

I couldn't believe it. A quick Google Map search of both of our addresses showed we lived 3-minutes-walk from each other. I stood up and looked out the window over my desk; the moon was almost full, covering our backyard in a pale white glow. The palm trees that separated our block from the neighbours behind us set creepy shadows across dad's shed.

I couldn't control the smile as I realised those neighbours were on the same street as Amber. She was across the road and up perhaps 200m. Her backyard would back onto the bushland that our bit of the suburb was built in to.

My laptop dinged a new message, bringing my attention back to its screen.

Amber: Well, now I know you're on my patch, you better watch your back.

Josh: Please, I've been here my whole life. You're in MY territory, girl.

Amber: Buddy, I'm a Camp Hill lifer, first and only house I've ever lived in. Either we arm wrestle this off, or we start counting the days between our Birthdays. I'm March 4.

Josh: Hey! That's the same day as Andy's! Sadly, though, that means it's my patch, not yours.

Amber: Dammit, February baby?

Josh: Nah, August, I thought we'd just agree younger models are better.

Amber: NO WAY THIS IS MY HOOD!

Josh: It's so weird to think we've spent basically 16 years this close and never met.

Amber: The world is all about timing Joshy, but you'll understand that when you're a bit older ;)

I smiled to myself and looked back out the window. The cold night air was quiet again, just the background white noise that comes with living in the suburbs. It was just Amber and I in this little bubble, passing away the hours, sharing more and more of our lives while the rest of the world slept.

Of course, it was not massively surprising that we'd live near each other — both our schools were in the same suburb that we lived in, though everyone called our little patch the "poor part." Dad gets so angry whenever I refer to it as poor though. As he constantly reminds me...and Mum...and really anyone who'll listen, "we're just 7km out of Brisbane's City, which is an absolute privilege."

Basically, thirty years ago, some developer who had mates in the city council paid off the right person so he could buy this little pocket of land and build a stack of houses on it. Before then basically every other house in the neighbourhood was built in the 1920s and had "character."

So when you come to our suburb, it's all beautifully restored old wooden Queenslanders... and then our patch of pretty much identical looking double-story boxes built by a very rich, connected Italian man who loved bricks.

Despite the ugly homes, our area is beautiful. We're right next to bushland that covers the biggest hill on our side of the city. It's riddled with tracks that take you on all sorts of walks through the hundreds of skinny trees and thick, towering gums that house koalas during the day, possums at night and birds at all hours.

Over the other side of the hill to our suburb is an old quarry that's slowly being rehabilitated into usable land. The quarry makes it look like some Godzilla sized creature came along and took a huge chunk out of the side of the hill - like it was ice-cream. Huge rock cliffs head straight down into the scarred base below after years of being cut away for road base.

Toward's the hill side of the quarry is a man-made lake we used to visit over the summer holidays as kids. Our parents gave us very stern warnings to never go in the water. It's deep and probably filled with dangerous chemicals.

The best part of our area, though, is the view from the top of the hill. From my place it takes around 45mins to climb to the top. Andy and I do it a couple of times a year. Thanks to years of digging away the other side while it was a quarry, there's an incredible ridge that has perfect views across the suburbs out to the city.

I reckon it's the most perfect, peaceful place in all of Brisbane. When you're up there, it's like you're on top of the whole city, but perfectly hidden away from everyone.

After realising we lived in the "poor part" together, Amber and I made plans to meet up for a special one-week reunion of our friendship after school on the coming Wednesday. Then, after hours of chatting, bird chirps heralded the first glimpses of daylight and we agreed it was well past bedtime.

I climbed into bed, absolutely exhausted, but buzzing with excitement. Amber was the coolest person I'd ever spoken to, and she spent a whole night giving her attention to me!

The five days between making plans and actually catching up felt more like five weeks, and then on Wednesday afternoon when the finish line was in sight, I had maths for my final period. Maths already felt like it dragged on forever, so the countdown to seeing Amber made it even worse.

My brain was swinging from excited to nervous. It still felt early enough in our friendship that I could say or do something stupid and ruin it all.

When the school day finally wrapped up, I couldn't even hold a conversation with people because I was so distracted by my thoughts. When I got home, I was too nervous to snack on anything, and even if I wanted to I barely had enough time to change, re-apply deodorant and make sure my hair didn't look lame school-boyish.

I looked up as I walked outside my house; the sky was the beautiful blue that winters bring with the sun being a little less scorching. A magpie was foraging for worms in my neighbour's yard. His mate watching on nearby, chortling a magpie song. This afternoon just felt perfect.

I'd probably walked past Amber's house 10,000 times in my life, but as I started up the hill this time, it was like seeing it for the first time. Suddenly this wasn't some random house around the corner. This is where Amber lived.

I fidgeted with my hair, and my clothes, and wiped my face as I slowly walked by her neighbours house, getting closer and closer to hers.

The door burst open as Amber emerged. I paused on her driveway trying not to seem too keen to see her, but then not wanting to be looking down at my phone like I was too important or busy. Then she spotted me and wandered down the flower lined path to her driveway, a cheeky grin on her face.

"Are you the Pizza boy?" She asked, before reaching out to give me a hug.

We wandered up Amber's street until we got to the little path leading into the walking tracks of the bushland. It was always a weird feeling as soon as you got just beyond the line of houses, suddenly surrounded by tall skinny trees and towering ancient gums. We were still in the middle of suburbia, but birds were singing and the breeze was wooshing.

I'd been nervous all day that we'd just run out of things to talk about, but our conversation flowed so easily. I felt myself starting to save conversations in my head to come back to as the topics moved so quickly. It was weird to think we'd only known each other for a week.

Time was passing way quicker then it felt. The sun was starting to set, slightly dimming the surrounding bush but painting the most incredible orange through the trees to the west. It was also starting to get cold. Brisbane was in that annoying time of the year when it was freezing cold in the morning before school, but by the time 10am rolled around wearing long pants meant my legs were uncomfortably dripping with sweat.

Right now I was regretting wearing gym shorts and was feeling a touch silly that Amber had the foresight to wear much warmer clothes.

I insisted we stop in a small clearing with a park bench before we turned around and headed home.

"It wouldn't be a real reunion without..." I teased, fishing in my backpack.

"If you've written me a card in your blood, this friendship is officially over," Amber dryly joked.

"Scotch finger biscuits!" I announced, presenting them in the air.

Amber squealed with delight and grabbed the packet off me, ripping them open and then breaking a biscuit in half, handing one finger to me and keeping the other before challenging me to a biscuit sword fight.

Two days earlier, when we decided to do this reunion, the first thought I had was "I need to do something cute and memorable." The Scotch Finger idea came almost instantly and I'm pretty sure it had worked exactly as planned.

After walking Amber back to her place, I had to stop myself sprinting home with the excitement I felt. I wandered home under the quickly darkening sky, watching the yellow streetlights awaken for the night and catching glimpses of the sounds of life from each home I passed. The smell of something tomatoey and garlicy from one kitchen, the voice of the TV newsreader beginning the bulletin with a very serious tone, and a car pulling into a driveway as a young kid slammed the door shut and complained about having to do homework.

The streets I'd grown up walking and riding my bike around had a new feeling tonight. I'd discovered something new and magical. Something that was just for Amber and I to enjoy.

———

Wednesday afternoon walks became our weekly thing. Within three weeks we'd started going twice weekly. Then my parents said we needed to have a "little chat" as we were finishing up dinner one night.

"Josh, all these walks, every afternoon, we'd like to know what you're getting up to?" Mum asked sternly.

"It's a senior thing!" I'd said, eyes rolling and all, "I'm in grade 12 next year and if I'm not focusing on my mental AND physical health it's not going to go well for me, is it!" I said pushing my chair out and picking up my plate - I could tell I was already starting to blush.

Mum stared at me with an eyebrow raised and a look that could have killed.

"I didn't come down in the last shower, Josh" mum replied, "sit back down and tell me where you're actually going. Even switched-on kids like you can end up in the wrong crowd."

"Wait, wait, WAIT," I said trying to sound really serious, "where the hell do you think I'm going?!"

"Josh, you know, we trust you mate," Dad continued, putting on a good cop voice, "but we're just worried about you, so if you tell us all you're doing is going out for a walk on your own... well, like I said, we trust you..."

I put my plate back on the table, sat down and exhaled. Mum was staring at me with a smile I knew was forced, trying so hard to show agreement with what Dad said, but memories from the past fresh in her mind.

They didn't need to worry about Amber and my walks, and they really didn't need to know about them at all. But I thought about how tightly some of my mate's parents monitor their kids and how Mum and Dad have never been like that with me, even though they had every reason to be.

I told them about meeting Amber at the social afternoon, and how when we realised we lived so close by we just decided to go for walks and how we're actually really good mates now. Smiles ripped across both of their faces and no matter how much I told them we were just friends, and no matter how much they assured me they understood, it was very clear they were convinced Amber was my girlfriend.

Mum insisted she meet Amber if our afternoon walks were going to continue, and I couldn't work out if she was worried Amber was going to a tattoo cover, motorbike riding, university student or if she was still convinced she was my girlfriend and she was keen to see what she was like. So after school the next day Amber walked over to my house, knocked on the door way more confidently than I ever would have and introduced herself to Mum.

I could tell mum was impressed, annoyingly she kept making comments about how great it was Josh had a girl friend, "like a friend friend, not a going on dates friend," she'd clarify as Amber laughed and I tried to hurry this horrible moment along!

Amber took me to meet her parents then. Honestly, I didn't fully understand why meeting the parents was such a thing that people worried about until that afternoon. I mean we weren't even dating - but I was terrified. I didn't need to be though. Amber's parents had seen me out walking with Amber and thought it was good she was getting out and about, not "sitting on her phone" all afternoon.

After successfully reassuring both sets of parents that we weren't buying drugs and stealing from old people to pay for our new habit, we managed to negotiate going for a walk every afternoon - as long as it was no more than 30 minutes on school days.

By this stage it honestly felt like we'd been in each other's lives forever. If we weren't out walking, we were messaging each other. During the day when something awesome or crappy would happen, my first thought was "Man, I need to tell Amber about this!"

There wasn't anything we didn't talk about. Except, of course, how much the boys were paying me out for being obsessed with her, and how Cal had basically told Andy that Amber was confused why I hadn't asked her out.

I had no idea how you'd ask a girl out anyway. Sometimes it felt like I'd missed some important stage between primary school and high school where you learn how to do these grown-up things - like asking a girl out on a date.

I'd sat in a class at school once and overheard some of the rugby boys talking about how they'd slept with a girl at a party over the weekend, but he and none of his mates could remember her name, or if any of them had ever been told her name. I sat there and wondered how on earth you can move from just meeting someone to sleeping with them in the same conversation. It honestly felt like watching a firefighter work out how to fight fires - like I get they're human and that they live in the same suburb as me, eat similar food to me, all that, and yet somehow they just have this whole set of knowledge that I don't even know where to begin with.

But late at night I'd lie in bed sure that if I didn't make some kind of move soon I'd be relegated to the friend zone, someone else would shoot their shot with Amber and this exciting, fresh time we'd shared together would dissolve into two people who wave at each other when they see each other at the supermarket a few times a year.

Eventually on one particularly sleepless night, staring out my window toward Amber's place, I came up with the ultimate plan to sweep her off her feet - we had to do a midnight sneak out.

4

FRIDAY NIGHT IS ALWAYS family games night at our house. Whoever won the week before gets to choose what takeout we get for dinner and what game we start on. I can literally only think of four times Dad, Mum and me haven't sat around our family dinner table and played some combination of Uno, Decision, Scrabble or Monopoly and one of those times I was in hospital and dad tried to argue with the nurse that I needed an IV taken out of my wrist so I could play.

On very rare occasions, a guest will be invited to join games night. On those occasions we play Cluedo and dad gets crazy competitive. When we were in primary school, my cousin Sammy was allowed to sleep over Friday nights on school holidays. After we played Cluedo, we'd build a blanket fort in the lounge room, eat huge amounts of sugar and stay up all night watching movies.

It's weird thinking of how close Sammy and I were in primary school. She was a year older than me and I remember hanging on every one of her stories the year she went off to high school, sucking up details that I hoped would make my time easier. I don't think we've exchanged more than a couple of words since I began high school.

Tonight, I chose Nandos for dinner after absolutely smashing Dad and Mum in Monopoly last week. There was no other option I could think of when the store became part of my daily planning for tonight's mission.

The 25min walk home from school each afternoon, up and down the hills of Chatsworth Road, had me deep in thought about how to perfectly pull off tonight's plan of asking Amber out. I'd taken so many notes on my phone - a few of them now seemed really lame, some impossible, but others struck me as pure genius.

At the street corner that connected our blocks to the rest of the suburb, there's a little row of shops that were built when our homes went up. Locals either love or hate the shops, mostly because the grocery store there is open 24/7 and Brisbane is one of those places that still has a real problem with places trading all night. The centre also has a chemist, Dominos Pizza and Nandos.

For the last week it has marked the end of my walk and was where my brain woke up out of "Sneak Out Mission" planning mode and switched into "OH MY GOSH I'M SO HUNGRY" mode. Every afternoon I'd see the Nandos and every afternoon I'd know it's all I wanted for Friday's victory dinner!

Once the Nandos was eaten, I told Dad and Mum that I only had enough brain power left for one game after a big week at school. This little white lie not only meant I'd be able to wrap things up quick enough to message Amber before she was tucked up in bed, but also meant my parents had no chance of suspecting me being up to no good late tonight - they'd be sure I was fast asleep.

I'd actually been trying to work out all week if I just tell them Amber and I were going for a late-night walk. They're actually cool with trusting me and I don't love the idea of sneaking out on them, but as I walked home this afternoon, I knew deep down that this would just be too close to their worst fears...I just knew they wouldn't be okay with this.

It was 9:55pm when I finally picked up my phone. Despite our sarcastic and witty banter, we were both getting worse at hiding how glad we were to chat with each other every night. Amber made it pretty clear she was glad I'd finally started replying to texts after basically being on read since 6pm.

I smiled to myself - this should make the plan work even better!

Josh: How much energy do you have tonight?

Amber: Hmmm normal, so glad that the weekend has finally arrived!

Josh: So I just thought of something a bit random...

Amber: Okay?

Josh: hmmm actually maybe it's a bad idea

Amber: Well, you can't do that!!! YOU HAVE TO TELL ME NOW, LOSER!!!

Josh: Bahahaha okay, but no pressure. You can say the idea is crazy and we shall never speak of it again haha.

Amber: Okay...

Now I was nervous. It felt like my whole body was numb with both excitement and nervousness and I wasn't in control of my typing anymore.

Josh: You up for a midnight sneak out and we can go hang out on the playground at the bottom of my street?

Amber: Haha, you are right, that idea is crazy

Amber: and stupid

Amber: and my parents would kill me

Amber: BUT I'm borrowing Cal's hoodie at the moment and I REALLY want an excuse to wear it... so I guess we don't really have a choice now, do we.

I literally jumped up from the couch with excitement!

"Josh, you okay?" Mum asked from the kitchen

"Yea yea, thought something was biting me but it's all good."

I had planned a little picnic basket with chocolate, strawberries and cookies, and some fake champagne. I had no idea how to ask a girl out and Google had been no help at all, so I decided to go as cute and as special as I could. Basically, I wanted to make sure when she told her friends about it that they were all impressed.

I didn't want Amber to be like that girl at the party that none of the boys could remember, even though they'd just shared this really intimate and close moment. I wanted to make sure that she had fun, that she was impressed, and that she felt like there was a big show put on because I wanted our relationship to be something important.

Google warned me this might actually put pressure on her.

But also, screw Google, it didn't help me when I asked "how do you know a girl isn't going to reject you."

———

I checked my phone again. Still 11:26. Less than a minute since Amber texted to tell me she was about to jump out her laundry window. It was downstairs in the back corner of her house and the furthest point from her parent's bedroom.

I'd been crouching in the bush at the corner of her backyard for five minutes. It was freezing cold, and I was not flexible enough for this. My leg was shaking. Also, I was sure someone must have seen me wander up the firebreak between the houses and the bushland, then sneakily hide in this bush and probably called the police to report a robber lurking around late on a Friday night.

Every slight rustle of leaves caused by the chilly midnight breeze made me think a snake was about to jump out of the bushes to attack me and this whole plan, my whole friendship with Amber, our potential future together was about to be ruined by a deadly snake biting me and her finding me dead in her garden in two minutes.

My heart raced a million miles an hour, and I nearly wet myself when I heard the sound of metal scraping coming from her house. Then through a window I saw the moonlit outline of Amber's face. I couldn't stop myself from smiling.

I watched Amber look down at the glow of her phone, tapping something away. Turns out it was a message to me.

Amber: If you jump out at me, I'm going to hit you in the head with a rock

Josh: I'm Josh's kidnapper, don't walk another step toward the bush in the corner of your backyard or I'll kill him.

I saw her face as she read the message. She smiled a cute smile, then looked up in my direction and said in a whisper, "Well if you're going to kill him I guess I'll keep walking this way then..." heading toward me with a wry smile. She was in a hoody, I'm assuming it belonged to Cal, with a single strand of her blonde hair poking out over the side of her face.

Amber became more fun and more adorable every time I hung out with her and I let my mind pray once more that she wouldn't reject me tonight.

We crouched in her backyard for another five minutes,

making sure her parents didn't stir and ensuring no neigh-bours were looking out the window, then we silently jumped the back fence and headed down the fire track toward the park.

"What's with the basket?" She asked when we were far enough away that there was no chance we would get grounded until we turned 30. "If I knew you wanted Scotch Fingers again I would have supplied this time! I'm a gal that can get her hands on the god tier snacks, Josh, don't doubt me!"

"This old thing?" I chuckled, slightly lifting the basket to show how heavy it was. "Oh, it's just my picnic basket ready for any late-night sneak out."

She gave a fake, over dramatic gasp, "do you do this with ALL the neighbourhood girls?"

Our arms bumped together, and I wanted so badly to grab her hand.

———

The playground had been recently upgraded by the city council and still smelt like new plastic. Right in the middle was some weird spinning thing - a big round piece of plastic that was shaped like a shallow bowl. Amber sat in it with the basket and I started spinning it around.

"JOSH!" she whispered, angrily but also giggling "I'm going to scream and people will think you're killing me and you'll go to jail and I don't want that," she said as she spun by me.

I grabbed the bowl, bringing it to a sudden stop, then climbed in with her.

The plastic was freezing cold, almost instantly zapping

through my hoodie, but there was nowhere else I'd have rather been.

"So! The basket!" I said, pulling it to me and opening it up, before laying each item in front of us. She clapped when the strawberries came out, and then grabbed the cookies and ripped them open before quickly putting one in her mouth and holding the packet to my face.

"You have to eat one now too," she said, through a cookie suspended between her lips. I picked one out.

We lay under the picnic blanket on the spinning thing, staring up at the stars, lazily eating strawberries and chocolate, our conversations getting gradually deeper and deeper as the time went on.

I angled my head closer towards hers and kept getting anxious about finding the right time to ask her out.

She told me about how when we graduate high school she wants to go to Cambodia and help girls who have been rescued out of sex trafficking. She'd watched a documentary that said there's more human slaves now than at any other point in history and sex trafficking is happening everywhere around us. I kept asking her question after question, knowing full well this girl was so smart and I desperately wanted to be at her level. I wanted to hear more of the things she'd heard and thought, and I wanted people to think of me the way I thought of her. Smart, mature, funny and so captivating.

Every sentence she spoke caught my attention and wouldn't let go.

I pulled my phone out and told her I wanted to see the trailer for this documentary. We lay there, heads pressed together, the stars behind my phone, her hand gently overlapping mine as we both held up the device.

As we watched, I could see the look in her eye. She was totally captivated by this story.

The next video on the screen was "10 Weird Beauty Trends"

"Hold up!" I exclaimed, "let me see how many of these I fit!"

The video started by talking about duck lips, the classic look of pouting out your lips that people did when taking a selfie.

"I'm great at this," I excitely exclaimed, before sitting up and turning to Amber with the most horrific attempt at a sexy pout that I could try.

She looked up at me, rolled her eyes, and then her face gave way to silent giggles, a snort and then a laugh that ripped through the entire park, echoing back to us.

"AMBER!" I whisper-yelled, secretly impressed with the reaction I got, as she covered her face, unable to stop laughing but mortified by the snort.

"I cannot believe I've already snort laughed in front of you!" She said after finally settling down.

I lay back next to her and let the video continue playing on my phone.

"Ohhh, thigh gaps," she said, mostly to herself, "Cal was telling us about this over summer."

The video explained a trend where girls would post photos of themselves standing with their legs together to see if there was a natural gap between the top of their thighs.

"So, was this like some kind of Cavendish College Gals summer fun of checking if they had a thigh gap?" I asked in a sarcastic voice.

"We didn't like post them or anything!" She replied with a smile, but a little defensive.

"Ohhh, did you have one, Amber?" I asked, keeping up my sarcasm, but secretly interested what she thought of it all.

"Nah, only Lauren did. She's so skinny," Amber said

29

dismissively, but then seemed to hold her breath for a second before continuing, "I wish we did it like when we were 12."

It was just a line, a quick sentence, but Amber said it in a way that made me realise this was a slight crack that led to much deeper thoughts; thoughts that made her feel a way she didn't want to feel.

From the day I'd met Amber she was the quickest, funniest, smartest, most interesting person in any conversation. In this moment it all disappeared and next to me lay a girl who was not sad, embarrassed or dramatic, but vulnerable, and I felt it hit me, slowly but with force.

I knew this conversation was not a regular one for her. I wondered if even Lauren and Cal had experienced it on the day, or if it was kept quiet only for these late-night moments where she'd already bared so much of her dreams, thoughts and ideas that there was no longer a filter telling her she must not let out her vulnerabilities.

"Well, I like this Amber, so I'm glad you're no different to who you are now," I said, unsure if it was the wrong thing to say, or too cheesy or Hollywood movie, but I was sure I meant it.

"Thanks" she smiled. Then, as if to change the topic as quickly as possible, she picked up the fake champagne and said, "Maybe I need to drink all my problems away," lifting the sealed bottle to her mouth and making big gulping noises.

We both laughed, trying hard to keep quiet as giggles filled the cool night air and our heads came back together side by side, lying down on the plastic.

"Okay, so my turn to share something I've been thinking about lots," I said to her, "I'm really worried about parties and drinking and drugs and all that."

"Okay," she replied cautiously, looking only slightly confused by where exactly I was going.

"I know Dan and Andy are getting more and more keen to go to parties and Dan is so into sneaking alcohol from his dad and getting drunk on Friday nights before going to bed, but I don't care for it. If anything, it scares me. It's like some weird thing that I don't understand and that I wish just didn't exist."

I was worried she was going to tell me how childish that was and how I needed to grow up.

"I get it," she said, nodding. "We all did it over summer. Lauren, Cal and I. Cal's sister gave us some raspberry flavoured vodka thing while her parents were away and I genuinely freaked out when Cal pulled them out of the fridge and handed them to us. I was thinking 'we don't do this, this isn't us, why are we having alcohol when we always have fun together?' I kinda said I wasn't that into it and Lauren gave me this weird speech about how I'd be a freak that doesn't go to parties and basically can't talk to boys unless I knew how to drink and not vomit everywhere."

"It's true," I replied, laughing a little, still trying to process the story, "basically as a guy I can't talk to girls that don't drink. My eight-year-old cousin just doesn't exist to me unless her dad gives her a mouthful of beer at family Christmas."

She laughed at me before continuing, "the funny part was that it turned out Lauren couldn't hold it, she basically ruined Cal's bathroom with non-stop vomiting while I could barely stand to help her out."

I hated this story, I hated it happened. Butterflies were filling my stomach as she talked. It was the same when Dan told me he was sneaking alcohol up to his room. I really liked my friends; I really liked Amber; I couldn't stand the thought of them being put in the danger that alcohol can so quickly force you in.

I knew sitting there with Amber in the freezing cold air that she'd shared so much of herself with me that I owed her my horrible story of getting drunk with people I trusted. I'd never told that story, or at least the full version, and I'm not sure I could.

I took a breath and started silently working out what to say first.

"Anyway, I was so scared I was going to have to find more friends or put up with getting drunk every time we hung out. Thank God we've never done it again, or even really talked about it," Amber's voice broke the silence of the night.

"Why'd you do it?" I asked, working hard to make sure my tone was curious, not judgemental. I needed to keep Amber going. I needed to find the right place to tell my story. I needed to work up the courage to start.

"Because I didn't have a choice, they'd hate me if I just sat there silently! Plus, being totally honest, too honest with you: it was the night of the thigh gap thing and Lauren was just lying there on the couch in a bikini with her thigh gap and flat stomach and I felt like a monster in a one piece and I couldn't deal with any judgement from them. The drinking kinda got rid of those thoughts...until Lauren started vomiting, then I just hated her for the rest of the night."

"But you see, I hated that even more! Why the hell did I need to take a drug to deal with something so small and stupid?" I could tell as Amber spoke that she'd thought about this before, probably a few times, and it made her feel stupid.

"First," I smiled, "you could be the only person outside of grade eight health teachers that calls alcohol a drug," we both laughed, "second, I think it's cool you actually thought

32

about that and realised that was going on. I don't reckon most people would. They'd just keep drinking to keep the feels away."

"Okay then, I have to ask," she said as she picked the fake wine back up, "if you hate alcohol than why the hell did you bring fake wine tonight?" Amber burst into a laugh.

She had a point. I lay back down, looking up at the stars and dramatically stretching my hands behind my head. "To celebrate our sneak out my dear, to celebrate our cunning plan" I said with a British accent.

She giggled, the giggle I heard the first time we met at Cavendish College, then lay down with her head resting on my arm, lightly touching my head.

The moment was gone. I owed her this story. I felt it in the pit of my stomach, but not tonight.

"I love how deep our conversations go, and that you ask questions that make me realise you actually listen... but THEN we can be laughing a second later. I love it so much," Amber whispered thoughtfully as we stared at the stars.

I wanted to reply with I LOVE YOU, AMBER, but I was sure that might forever ruin my chances with any girl ever from Cavendish College and earn me the nickname Stage 100 clinger.

The time to open up about that horrible night was gone.

This moment, though, this was it, it was now or never. I felt butterflies surge to my tummy again and words bubble in my chest.

"Amber?" I said, nervously, then lay in silence, so unsure of what to say next.

"What?" she said, slightly alarmed. Perhaps I'd been too serious. When I didn't reply instantly, she got on her elbow and looked at me, "What's up?"

"Will you be my girlfriend" I asked, as cutely as I could.

"Oh my gosh!" She gushed, with a big smile on her face,

"I thought you were about to tell me you were suffering some terminal disease or something!"

"I will be depending on what you say next!" I laughed back at her.

"Yes, yes definitely! Of course!" She replied, laughing back at me and awkwardly putting a hand on my chest.

"Yesss. Girlfriend Acquired." I said, excited, whispered and really just because I didn't know what else to say. I felt excitement rush through my whole body and suddenly I had way too much energy for this time of night.

"Girlfriend acquired?" She giggled as she tried to stare at me with an unimpressed look, before lying back down next to me, holding my hand, staring at the stars. They seemed brighter now.

"Cute date, by the way," she said and squeezed my hand.

"I'm worried I started too strong and won't be able to follow it up now!" I replied, "but hey, at least your friends will remember this and then no guy will ever be good enough for them."

"Way to make a girl feel special. Here I was thinking this was all just for me..." she said with a cheeky smile.

"Shut up Amber!!! I've been thinking about this from like the day we met, this is all you!"

We laughed and chatted until my phone said it was 3.30, then we began wandering back across the field towards home.

As we got to the middle, lit by the moon, both our heads covered by our hoods to protect us from the freezing night breeze, I grabbed Amber's hand and pulled her into me for a hug.

Then I leaned back, looking down at her, the stray strand of hair over the left side of her face again. She looked up at me curiously, her eyes wide, skin looking so soft. I can't believe we'd only known each other for a month and now, staring at her face, I couldn't imagine a world where I didn't talk to her every day.

All I wanted to do was kiss her. I thought after I asked her out it would all be so natural, but this was so much scarier. She was so wonderful and had so many friends that were boys. I was sure she'd have kissed someone much cooler than me before and if my kiss sucked she'd instantly regret saying yes to me, worrying she'd be stuck with such a horrible kisser.

Maybe on Monday her, Cal and Lauren would laugh about how bad I was and therefore how terrible I'd be at doing other stuff, and how I should be dumped as soon as possible.

"What?" she asked me, so sweetly, looking up with her beautiful eyes, curious about why we were just standing looking at each other.

"I want to kiss you so much," I blurted out, then awkwardly laughed.

"Then do it!" She said shyly, but developing a cheeky smile, "but I've never been kissed before, okay, so it's going to be bad."

I smiled a purposely wry smile, wanting to give the impression I was in control of this. I'd teach her the ropes, but my nerves got the best of me and I quickly blurted out "Neither, this should be interesting."

Before I knew it, my face was slowly moving toward hers and we kissed gently. Her lips were so soft and her breath so warm. We separated by just an inch, pausing for a moment. I wanted more. It was the most perfect feeling I had ever felt. We kissed gently again. This time I tried opening my lips a little, and she responded with the same, suddenly closing them. I quickly matched her, then we opened again. I honestly hadn't thought this needed to be done, the opening and closing, but it made so much sense and felt so good. My arms were around her waist, hers around my neck, her hair occasionally getting in the way but pushed aside with little giggles. This was the most perfect moment I'd ever had.

There was saliva everywhere, but when we finally pulled away, we both had huge smiles on our faces.

"We need to get better at that," she said through her smile.

"Well, we better get in as much practise as we can," I grinned back at her.

We continued our walk home, hand in hand.

5

AMBER and I went for a walk almost every afternoon after we became "official," even on Saturdays and Sundays. One week it rained for three days non-stop, so I arrived at her house carrying an umbrella and two big bin bags.

"Are you planning to clean up rubbish as we walk?" Amber said, confused.

"NO! The umbrella is great, but look at my pants, they're soaking wet - we're going to have to wear the rubbish bags if we don't want to get wet... BUT, I don't want to be seen like this, so we'll have to walk through the bushland," I said, holding a rubbish bag out to her.

"Okay, but show me how first," she said, looking at me with a cheeky grin.

It was only as I'd made leg holes and started pulling the bag up I saw her holding back a laugh.

"What?!"

"We are NOT walking in the bush in this rain," she said. I looked up at the trees behind her house and realised how muddy and wet it would be in there.

"Also, I'm not wearing a garbage bag you loser!" She laughed at me. Then, at the worst possible moment, her dad's car roared through puddles up the street and turned into the driveway next to us.

"Nice outfit, Josh," Amber's dad said, his window wound down just a little to prevent himself getting wet, "and how nice of you to bring an umbrella for my daughter... just a real shame she'd never want to be seen with a guy in a garbage bag!" He wound up his window and moved up the driveway into the garage.

"He's right...." Amber said, breaking into a smile.

We both burst into laughter. I moved under the umbrella with her, pulled her into me and kissed her deeply.

"HEY! Back off bin bag boy!" Her dad yelled from the garage as he closed the door.

We laughed as we kissed, then went for a very soggy wet walk.

There was no small talk on our walks, and I regularly shared things that I'd be too embarrassed to share with anyone else - like how stupid I felt that I had put no time into maths again, the subject I always failed, so I failed yet another assignment. It always made my parents angry, and I felt so guilty about it, but they seemed to think I didn't even care.

One afternoon we were debating if Futurama or The Simpsons was funnier when Amber suddenly started to cry.

"Urghh, sorry," she said, fanning her face and looking embarrassed about the sudden tears.

"Oh, what's wrong, Amber?" I helped her sit down on the beautifully manicured front lawn of some random house in the neighbourhood.

"It's nothing," she took a deep breath in, stilling her tears. "It's been a big week with band rehearsal. Every lunchtime I've got something else on and I'm just not catching up with everyone, you know?"

"Sure," I smiled at her. She stared into the distance, physically right next to me but mentally a million miles away. "Did something happen?"

"Yes. Well no. It's just Lauren." Her tears started up again. "Every time I finally get a chance to see everyone Lauren just carries on with everything I've missed. Like if someone brings up something that was talked about when I wasn't there and I even laugh Lauren will like death stare me and say 'You weren't even here, why are you laughing.' And she just... I don't know."

I pulled Amber in for a hug. I was at a loss of what I could say or do and I hoped that just being here to listen was enough. Cars drove down the street and people awkwardly looked at us as they passed. I realised this was usually the kind of situation I'd find embarrassing, but in this moment all I could think about was the pain Amber was feeling and how desperately I wished I could fix it in some way.

"She calls me fat, basically," Amber suddenly said into my chest.

"What?!" I replied, feeling both shock and anger. Of course Amber was not fat. It was completely untrue. But who would even say something so blunt and horrible.

"She doesn't actually call me fat, she just started saying I was stress eating and then today at lunch she made some comment like 'Wow, Amber, are you really eating all that?'"

I held Amber tighter. She was crying deep heavy sobs now. I was so disgusted by how obvious and horrible Lauren's attacks were. Why was she being so horrible?

"You're so beautiful," I told Amber, kissing her on the top of her head.

As the term started to come to an end and exams were about to start, Amber and my walks sometimes turned into a quick hug and five-minute check in as the two of us tried to get through our huge study loads. Some evenings Amber would text and say she had to leave her phone out in the kitchen so she'd actually concentrate and not get distracted. It was so weird how hard it was to go four hours through the night without hearing from her.

The Friday afternoon in the middle of our two-week exam block, we'd set aside to go for a long walk through the bush.

"One week till holidays!" Amber said after we both unloaded about how unnecessarily stupid giving grade eleven's this much work was.

"Isn't it funny how one week can feel like it's so impossibly far away! What's your plans for the break?" I asked.

"Sleep...sleep more...and then I'll get out of bed just to feel the joy of getting back into it," Amber replied with a gleeful smile across her face. "But actually, not many plans at all. I think some of the girls want to do a Harry Potter marathon to celebrate the one-year anniversary of the last movie coming out. What about you?"

"Also, absolutely nothing. Andy and I try to go bowling every Tuesday of school holidays because we like to pretend we've got really important traditions, but other than that I plan to get well acquainted with my TV."

"Bowling! Oh my gosh, I don't reckon I've gone bowling since I was like ten. I'm messaging Cal - her and I are definitely coming."

"O EM GEE DOUBLE DATE!" I exclaimed, mustering my best impression of an excited teenage girl.

"YESSS DOUBLE DATE!" Amber replied, excitedly

grabbing my hands. I leant in and kissed her. Butterflies filled my stomach and I didn't want to pull away. I still couldn't believe that I was dating Amber, and it was moments like this that I realised how lucky I was.

"Kissing you never gets old," I told her.

"I feel the same," she whispered, smiling and leaning up to kiss me one more time.

"By the way!" I said, keeping one hand holding hers but swinging my body out to keep our walk going. "My dad is way too keen for you to come to family games night. Maybe school holidays could be the time? If you're up for it, of course! If it's just too weird, I can totally make excuses for you!"

"Are you KIDDING?" she asked, a huge grin across her face, "I actually thought I'd have to marry you before I was invited to family games night! The fact that Simon and Pauline are going to let me be part of family games night now is huge!"

"I mean, if you call them by the first names, the invite is rescinded..." I laughed, relieved by her excitement, and terrified by how awkward this could be.

"Please Josh, Simo and Leeny love me!" She smiled up at me and winked. "Oh, I want to bring dessert! A cake maybe? Let's cook a cake and take it for dessert!"

"Also! Have you ever been up to the top of the hill? We should walk up there over the holidays!"

"Yes! You know what we need?" Amber stopped walking, looking excitedly with her hands out in front of her as if her idea needed room, "a relationship bucket list! All the ideas and things we want to do together, written on a handy dandy list!"

"I flipping love it!" I replied, "why are you even doing exams Amber? You're clearly way too clever already!"

· · ·

The relationship bucket list ended up saving me over the next week of exams. Every few hours, one of us would think of another thing and message it with the item number we were up to. Amber's final exam was two days before mine, so she designed this epic poster with all the bucket list items on it.

JUNE 2012

6

───────

AMBER AND CAL crashed our Tuesday morning ten-pin bowling session on the first week of the June/ July school holidays. We awkwardly realised the night before that it was actually Amber and my first official date. A double date.

Andy and I bounded up the stairs of the Greenslopes Bowling alley, both a bit louder and more animated than usual, knowing that Cal and Amber were watching us from the foyer.

"So Cal and Andy have played together before," Amber informed me after exchanging our hellos, "if we lose it'll be unfair, just saying it in advance."

"Well, actually," Andy jumped in boldly, "It's boys verse girls."

Amber looked up at me wide-eyed and questioning this plan.

"Sorry babe," I told her, "I gotta rep with ma boy."

"Be whiter," she said and rolled her eyes, smiling slyly.

Andy had raised this on the bus coming here: one of the really interesting parts of his and Cal's relationship was that it started from this place of great friends. After Amber and I started dating, they realised they probably should stop the games and at least try it and mostly, it actually seemed to work for them. But they were still hilariously competitive and way too comfortable with each other.

All our friends called Amber and I the "In love honey-mooners" and Andy and Cal the "Couple married for 50 years." I liked it.

Andy and I won the first game convincingly, 182 to the boys, 109 to the girls, which resulted in claims that we weren't chivalrous and that real men would have let their girlfriends win.

"Nup," Andy pronounced, "This is equality, Cal" he said before turning and going to collecting his ball.

"Josh, you're playing with me," Amber said in a tone made it clear this was definitely not up for discussion.

"Alright!" I said, plenty of excitement in my voice so Andy wouldn't contest it. Instead he just made a whipping noise.

Game two was much harder for my competitive side. Cal and Andy were superb at bowling. In fact, it could be argued I was holding Andy back in game one as they hit 200 before the game even finished. Knowing we had no chance, Amber and I started trying our own styles, only settling down when the angry manager came over smelling like old deep-fryer oil and told us we'd be asked to leave if Amber bowled while I had her over my shoulder again. On one hand he seemed a bit like the fun police, but also...the ball had ended up in the next lane over and almost definitely ruined a very competitive looking man's bowl.

Cal and Amber went for a toilet break a few bowls in to game two. As Andy and I waited for them at our lane, the early 2000s soundtrack blaring through the alley switched to Avril Lavigne's *Sk8er Boi* and the two of us started reciting the lyrics to each other as if it was a story. I looked around, took a breath in and realised how much I loved this moment. If this is what my life with Amber, Cal and Andy in it was going to be like, I hoped things would never change.

———

Not long after the girls returned, Amber excitedly ran back behind the lane and threw her arms around Matt Coulson. I had no idea they'd even met, but they were getting along like old friends reuniting. Instantly, I felt uncomfortable. Not jealously. I trusted Amber as someone that would be honest and keep their word more than anyone I'd ever met, but Matt was the complete opposite. Probably the biggest drop-kick of our grade.

He wasn't a "beat you up for your lunch" kind of bully, but he definitely didn't make many people feel good being around him. One time, three weeks into grade eight - before I even knew his name - he and his mate stopped in the stairway while passing me, pointed and said, "This kid looks like a dinosaur, hey? He's just so ugly."

I was shocked for the rest of my afternoon, trying to work out what the hell even happened there or what I'd done that had made them turn on me like that.

Six months later I learnt his name when he got suspended for bringing alcohol to school and leaving it in the quiet nerdy kid in his maths class' bag. Matt had proceeded to pull out the alcohol in front of a teacher to see if he could, and I quote, "get the nerd in trouble."

"Got another strike buddy..." Andy distracted me with his smug voice and tap on the shoulder.

"Ohhhhh... this isn't like golf?" I asked him sarcastically, "We're meant to be going for the highest score?" When I looked back to Amber, she was bouncing back down to the lanes.

"You're back?" I asked with a smile.

"Couldn't let you have my go now, could I? I'd be worried the manager would kick us out for that too!" she quipped as she picked up her ball.

I looked back to where Matt and Amber had been standing moments ago. Matt was staring at me with a look of disgust. I tried smiling and nodding to him, but he just shook his head, turned and walked away.

I felt gross.

I was still awkwardly standing, staring at where Matt had been when Amber jumped on my back, kissed my cheek and yelled "I got a strike, stallion!"

"REALLY!" I excitedly met her energy and galloped over to where Andy and Cal were, before noticing the scoreboard saying she'd only knocked one pin down. She jumped off my back.

"Yea! Like as in, I've knocked down ten pins this entire game!" She laughed. I high fived her before turning to Andy and Cal.

"You two better watch out, Amber might knock down 20 pins total this game!"

———

After we'd had our butts handed to us, Andy and Cal, or "The Champions" as they'd asked us to call them for the rest of the game, were versing each other on the arcade games in the back of the bowling alley while Amber and I sat and ate hot chips.

"How do you know Matt Coulson?" I ask her while trying to chew a chip that was clearly burning my mouth.

"Can I just say, that view of chewed food in my

boyfriend's mouth is absolutely superb!" she giggled, before taking a big chip in her mouth to impersonate me, then realising her mistake as the heat burnt her mouth, "oh crap!" She said, wide-eyed surprise but smiling at her mistake.

I poured water into her mouth from my drink bottle. "Here! This will save you!"

She swallowed, laughing, "wow, what a hero, giving me soggy chips!"

"Babe, I swear to always make your chips soggy," I said in a pretend romantic voice.

"Ewwww! That SOUNDS gross!" She burst into laughter.

"Music camp last year!" She continued, "Matt and I started chatting at dinner one night. He's a really sweet guy!"

"He's an arsehole," I replied.

"Oh, I thought you were friends. He was joking around like you two were mates?" She replied.

"Maybe I read him wrong," I said, surprised, "but I'm pretty sure he hates me."

It scared me a little that someone who'd been pretty standoffish with me in the past was apparently good friends with Amber. It scared me he'd make me look like an idiot or make her think I wasn't good enough for her.

I wondered how often they talked, what he'd said about me and if he'd planted any seeds of doubt about me to Amber. I'd obviously been looking as anxious as I felt because Amber reached out and put her hand on mine.

"I'm not interested in him, Josh," she told me calmly.

"No, I know," I replied, "I'm just scared of something ruining this."

"Don't be," she said before reaching up to put her hand under my chin, then said in a fake parental encouraging tone, "chin up kid, ain't nobody taking away my walking buddy."

I laughed and leant over to kiss her.

"WOOOP, WOOOOP PDA ALARM!" Andy yelled from across the room as he and Cal walked back over to us.

"We got 400 tickets, we're getting bouncy balls, you losers can get back to your kissing," he proudly announced, "ready to play with my balls Cal?" He crudely asked. She rolled her eyes.

"Please, his balls basically live in my trophy cabinet," she said to us and winked.

7

"Amber! Of English origin, meaning 'to assess whether one should stop or go. derived from traffic lights'," my dad pronounced as we sat down for games night dinner, featuring Amber. I think you could actually hear my eyes roll.

"Actually Mr. Matherson, I'll have you know its French origin and I milk that for every bit of sophistication I can get!" Amber replied, beaming up at my dad.

"Ha!" I said, looking at my dad trying to rub in Amber was way wittier than him.

"Oh! I like her! I like her a lot!" He looked at me with a giant smile across his face. "Tonight we play Pictionary!" Dad raised his glass, clinking it with mum as they tasted the wine Amber brought over for them.

"A good drop from a great family!" Dad declared, referring to Amber's mum insisting she bring the wine as a guest at our home. Our plans to bake a cake had been thwarted when we got tricky and put food dye in the cake. The cake then didn't rise because we kept opening the oven to check it's colour. Needless to say, a grey lump didn't seem like an appropriate dessert to present my parents.

We tucked into Afghan food from a restaurant a suburb or two over, when I told Amber that my parents wanted her to choose the meal I thought she'd do the faux polite thing and say she wanted us to choose something we all liked, but she went straight for it. I just loved how easy and real every part of our relationship was - I didn't have to worry about Amber faking it to make me happy.

After dinner, mum brought out heaps of lollies and chocolate as dad set-up Pictionary.

"Wow! What a spread, mum!" I said, eyeing off the massive haul she was laying out on the table.

"Well, we have a special guest," she said, smiling at Amber. "This takes me back to the days when Sammy would spend Friday nights with us." she looked at me with a tight smile. I briefly returned it, then made a grab for the TimTams.

"Have you done a TimTam slam?" I asked Amber, noticing that she was still caught on trying to work out who Sammy was. I hoped she hadn't sensed the awkwardness in that exchange.

"You mean bite the two ends off and then dunk it in tea and suck it up through the biscuit?"

"YES! Hot chocolate or tea? I'm going to make them now."

I watched from the kitchen as Amber chatted with my mum, telling her about school and her plans for after graduation. I could literally see her face light up as she talked about her dream of travelling to Cambodia and working with girls rescued out of sex trafficking. I quickly sent her a message that I knew she wouldn't see until the end of the night:

Josh: #27 *Live in Cambodia, working with trafficked girls.*

I'd always wanted to travel after I graduated. I'd always

been excited about owning and running a restaurant one day, so I'd started thinking it'd be cool to get a job in one of the Michelin star restaurants in London, Paris or even Spain. Obviously at like dish pig level. I think you have to basically be a world famous chef to even be a waiter in most of those places. But the more Amber told me about her dream to help end the trafficking of young girls, the more I wanted to be part of doing that with her. It's like the deeper I fell for Amber, the deeper the things she cared about mattered to me. I wasn't just falling for Amber the person, but everything that came with her, right down to her thoughts and passions.

As I grabbed the two mugs of hot chocolate and began walking back to the living room, I realised mum was now showing Amber an old photo of Sammy and I. Meanwhile dad had apparently left the room to deal with... who knows what! My stomach sunk.

"Your mum was just telling me about your cousin Sammy!" Amber said, looking up at me as I handed her a mug. Her facial expression changed to uncertainty as she talked, and I realised I was wearing frustration on my face.

"Ah, awesome," I said, faking a smile.

"I was telling her about all the holidays we went on together. How you two were inseparable right through primary school. All the sleepovers - remember when you used to record yourselves pretending you were on the radio?" Mum said with a sense of nostalgia in her expression.

"So, did she move away in high school or something?" Amber asked.

"Nah, she's at Cavendish College - you might know her - Samantha White?" I replied, hoping to steer the conversation away from any story about why Sammy didn't come over anymore.

"Oh maybe? Is she sporty? I feel like she's been up on assembly before?"

"Yep! That'd be her!" I replied as dad wandered back in from the bathroom.

"So why haven't I met this wonderful Sammy? Where has your childhood bestie disappeared to?" Dad looked at me, surprised hearing the question, and I quickly flicked my eyes to mum with a clenched jaw. A disappointed look came across his face.

"Guess we just grew our separate ways," I said with a smile to Amber. She smiled backed and nodded, understanding that this was not something I wanted to address here.

"Well, I think Josh is embarrassed about something he did and isn't ready to talk to Sammy about it yet..." mum continued meekly, apparently aware this would not be appreciated by me yet somehow unable to stop herself. I felt anger surge through me as I looked up at her trying to pull a face that shouted "SHUT UP NOW!"

"Pictionary time, Amber!" Dad quickly interrupted as Amber looked at me a little confused. I grabbed her hand and squeezed. "Now, just because you're a guest that brought us great wine doesn't mean we're going to go any easier on you. One of the great bits of wisdom I've taught young Josh his entire life is that Pictionary is the ultimate game to find out how close people are - being married is such an advantage that it's almost a cheat, so don't feel bad when you lose."

"Dad, you and mum have LITERALLY never won a game!" I threw at him, avoiding any eye contact with mum. I couldn't work out what she was getting at with bringing the whole Sammy saga up tonight, in front of Amber.

"Since you've been born! Before you came in and took

all our brain cells away, we were unstoppable!" Dad said without missing a beat.

Watching Amber playing Pictionary as part of the most sacred tradition of my family was so cool. After the first round I'd stopped feeling mad at mum, and I'm so glad I let it go. The four of us basically laughed the whole way through the game. Amber was unafraid to be totally herself, and all the in-jokes we'd shared meant we were pretty great at working out each other's clues, even with my terrible drawing.

"Oh come ON! There's no way you could have got beard from a picture of a dog!" Mum exclaimed through laughter. She and dad were sitting on the couch, Amber and I were across the coffee table from them sitting in a fort of all the pillows from around the downstairs of my house.

"First," I replied, a lolly snake hanging out of my mouth. "That's a goat, not a dog."

"It's so obvious now..." Dad replied sarcastically while looking conspicuously on our side of the table to see if we'd found a way to pass notes to each other.

"My maths teacher looks like one of those shaggy mountain goats," Amber continued my explanation, "And also has the most disgusting beard! That is pretty much all anyone notices about him."

"Oh, my Lord!" Mum replied, rolling her eyes but starting to get the giggles. Amber and I had lost it in fits of laughter on the floor now. "Honestly, teachers deserve millions of dollars a year for having to put up with you teenagers."

If Dad's Pictionary theory is right then Amber and I know each other pretty well, and after watching how perfectly she fits in with my family, I couldn't be more excited about that.

"It's an open invite for you Amber, please come by any Friday night," Dad said as he and mum called it a night and headed for bed just after 10:30.

"Absolutely Amber, I'd love to see you around more!" Mum continued with a genuine smile.

"Thanks Mr and Mrs Matherson, I had so much fun with you guys."

"No seriously Amber, even if you break up with Josh and it's awkward we can send him to his grandparents or something, we'd just love to see you..." dad continued with a smirk.

"Boooo," I yelled from the couch, throwing a lolly snake up at him, "go to bed old man."

"Why are you so great to be around all the time?" I asked Amber. She smiled and let her head fall into my lap as she lay across the couch.

"No, really I organise all these tests to try to break you and you just keep impressing..." I joked as I stroked her hair.

"I love you, Josh..." she said.

"I love you too, Amber," and I did.

"That was a first." She looked up at me with her beautiful, big, innocent eyes. I kissed her on the forehead.

Perhaps Hollywood had made me think that saying "I love you" for the first time was meant to be a big moment with days of thought and checking if you really meant it before you said it, but with Amber it was the most obvious and honest thing I felt. There was no big moment of realisation, no fireworks in my tummy, just the slow, day by day fall into knowing that nothing happened in my day that I didn't want to share with Amber.

Amber pulled her phone out of her bag, her screen filled with notifications. I watched her click on my name first.

"Seriously?" She sat bolt upright, an excited, unfakeable smile across her face. "You'd do a gap year in Cambodia with me? Like you'd actually want to do that?"

"Hell yeah!" I replied, "everything you've told me has broken my heart! If we could do something, ANYTHING, why wouldn't we? PLUS it's super cool watching you do things you're really passionate about. I'd be happy just to watch you do something you're so happy about for a year."

"Joshua!" Amber said, launching toward me with a tight hug, kissing me deeply, then looking me straight in the eyes, our faces barely an inch apart, "why are you so great to me all the time!"

"Because you deserve it," I lightly kissed her on the lips, then our faces lingered, barely separated. The electricity in the air around us was buzzing as I felt her gentle breath on my face. She kissed me deeply again, and I pulled her body close to me, so desperate to have as much of my body physically touching hers.

"Woooo!" Amber exhaled as we separated, her face was flushed. She went back to checking the other notifications on her phone, her free hand still playing with my hair.

"Oh no!" Amber's eyes widened and a look of worry overtook her.

8

"Is everything okay?" My stomach dropped as my mind tried to grasp at what could be wrong.

"Bella just got dumped by Joe," Amber continued, reading through what looked liked paragraphs and paragraphs of text.

Bella was one of Amber's friends from school - I'm not sure they were best friends, but they had a few classes together and were getting closer. From the stories Amber told me, it sounded like Bella had a wicked "my life is a mess but I'm okay with it" sense of humour.

"Oh, that sucks," I said, sympathetically but unsure how big of a deal this was. "How long have they been together?"

"I'm pretty sure for a long time. She said something the other day about them being family friends and they just kind of always have been dating as long as they can remember." Amber was distracted flicking through the notifications from Bella.

"Oops, she tried to call me a couple of times earlier."

"Where's she live?" I casually asked, a memory of Amber pointing out her house on a walk a couple of weeks ago. "She the one up the road?"

"Yea! She's my walking home pal!" Amber looked up at me. "I should take flowers or something to her house tomorrow morning, hey?"

"I've got one better," excitement shot through me and I couldn't keep it out of my voice, "lets go down the road now, get a heap of like chocolate, ice cream, lollies, whatever and just rock up on her doorstep with it!"

Amber lifted her hand up to high five me, an adventurous look running across her face as she nodded slowly.

"Brilliant Josh, absolutely brilliant!"

The night air was freezing - each gust of wind felt like ice hitting my skin and the warm breath leaving our bodies instantly turned into mist making it look like we were smoking. But we were back out. As the neighbourhood slept around us Amber and I were back on a late-night adventure.

"I love being out late at night," I loudly whispered to Amber as we walked down the middle of my deserted street, excitement pulsing through me.

"I love the adventures we go on!" Amber whispered back.

As we wandered through the carpark Amber was distracted by a cat running into a drain next to the store's entry. As she shrieked how gross it was that someone's family cat was spending the night in the drain, she didn't see the gutter and tripped forward, saving herself with a little run right before she hit the ground.

This sent both of us into fits of laughter as we entered the bright lights of the nearly empty store. An unimpressed girl, probably only a few years older than us, was working behind the cigarette counter and stopped flicking through her phone to give us a very unimpressed glare.

"M'lady," Amber said, pretending to tip a top hat on her

head toward the woman, who rolled her eyes and shook her head.

"Sorry," I mouthed, trying to give the impression that Amber was just having a weird night. Fear ran through the back of my mind that the worker would demand to call our parents if we were too loud and disturbed the eerie peace of the late night supermarket.

We quickly made our way to the ice cream fridges on the far side of the store. The store was pretty much empty - just two aisles with actual shoppers in them, and one with a staff member restocking shelves, occasionally clattering a can on the shelf and disturbing the awkwardly loud sound system playing Maroon 5's song "She Will Be Loved."

"I just wish I could find me a guy that treats me like this," I said with my best impression of a girl as the song reached the chorus.

Amber looked back at me, that look of adventure still plastered across her face and a cheeky smile developing, "Isn't this song about a prostitute?"

"Are you seriously going to ruin classic Maroon 5 with that uneducated statement!" I pretended to be disgusted.

"Wait, wait, that's Ed Sheeran's The A-Team," she dramatically hit herself in the head.

"Oh yeah, that girl has some real issues," I replied with a pretend look of concern. "Can't help thinking she's the kind of girl that would be in the ice cream aisle of a supermarket at like 11:30 on a Friday night..." I stared sarcastically at Amber.

"Honestly, who the hell is doing their grocery shopping at midnight on a Friday?" Amber asked, throwing her hands in the air, then from the next aisle over we heard someone abruptly clear their throat.

Both of us looked at each other, mouths open, shocked,

and trying so hard to keep our fits of laughing silent as we bumped into each other.

"I mean, what wonderful, clever people avoiding crowds like that..." I said purposely, a bit too loud, with mock seriousness in my voice.

We were in the store until just after midnight. From the conversation we overheard, the two employees clearly were unimpressed with us. My stomach tossed and turned as my fear that they were calling security or going to ask us to leave or something resurfaced. Amber reassured me that they were probably tired uni kids who didn't want to put up with the annoying, noisy crap of two high school kids, then encouraged me to keep being annoying and noisy.

We left with three bags full of chips, chocolate and ice cream, as well as a small platter of carrot and celery sticks with hummus.

"The greatest lesson I can teach you about teenage girls, Josh, is that you don't know if their emotional breakdown food is actually hummus," she said before booping me on the nose with the carrot stick bag.

———

Bella met us at the front door with puffy, bloodshot eyes and a tear-stained face. She wore flannelette pyjama pants and a grey shirt with bold black letters that said "Forget party rock, I'm in the house tonight."

Amber handed over the bags of snacks while introducing me. Bella whispered how great we were, that all she had wanted tonight was chocolate and quickly added that we can't wake her parents up.

"Ha! As in Party Rock Anthem? The LMFAO song?" I

said, pointing to her shirt, a little bit uncomfortable with the tears and feeling out of my depth about comforting a girl who had just been dumped.

"Yes," Bella replied, her face scrunching up as her shoulders dropped and deep sobs took over her whole body. "Joe got it made for me because I always said that when I arrived at his house."

Amber pulled Bella into a hug, shaking her head and giving me a cheeky smile. I put my head in my hands and stepped away to give the girls some space.

I flicked through random things on my phone for a few minutes before Bella's whispered, angry explanation of what Joe had done was wrapping up. They hugged each other goodbye as I looked up.

"Sorry for scaring you, nice to meet you!" Bella whisper-yelled over to me, with the tiniest bit of extra joy in her expression.Amber certainly had a way of making people feel good.

"Enjoy the Tim Tams!" I whisper-yelled back as Amber made her way back across to me.

We watched Bella close her front door, then walked hand in hand down the street.

"Of COURSE I point out the shirt that CLEARLY had a backstory!" I whispered dramatically once we were safely away from Bella's.

"Oh my gosh Josh, why are boys so clueless!" She said, letting go of my hand and lightly hitting me over the back of the head.

"You're a great friend Amber. It felt like you were the only person she wanted to talk to tonight." I grabbed her hand again and pulled her close to me, lightly kissing her on the forehead. She looked up at me with her bright beautiful eyes and smiled.

"I love you," I told her.

"I love you, too," she replied.

Then all at once she pulled me up the street in the opposite direction of her place.

"Babe, you've forgotten where you live," I sarcastically told her as she dragged me along the street.

"You've been up to the top of the hill before, hey?" She asked, still powering forward.

"I've lived here my whole life! Of course I have!" I said, realising that was where she was taking us and secretly hoping the fact I've been there before meant she'd turn around and head home.

"It's stunning there at night," she continued, "let's head up there! Our next late night adventure!"

Usually late night adventures would have excited me - that was the awesome way we started dating after all - but late night, adventure, and being that close to the old quarry put a pit in my stomach.

"This feels like a bad idea..." I said as we walked down the pathway into the bush.

"Josh, we're bigger and scarier than anything hiding in this bush!" Amber replied, full of unquestionable confidence.

"Oh boy, I didn't even think about what could attack us. I more meant the getting lost, or getting hurt," I tried to find good reasons that weren't clearly made up excuses.

"Really? My eyes feel like they've totally adjusted. I can see fine, plus we'll just check Google Maps on our phone if we can't work out how to get back," Amber replied, more confused by my hesitancy than anything else.

She was right too - the trail up to the summit was wide and well marked. The council had just finished upgrading the trails in March, lining them with rocks to ensure animals couldn't mess up the edges. Plus, Andy and I walked these trails so regularly that I could basically draw the map to the top. The classic fear of stumbling into the path of a dangerous animal (or some kind of criminal activity) never really struck me doing this walk, maybe because I'd done it so many times, and tonight the moon was bright enough that there basically weren't any more shadowy places than there would be in the day.

I looked up. This bushland wasn't some dense jungle, the tree trunks were mostly skinny with a few towering gum trees every so often. Birds were calling, occasionally possums would screech at each other and animals would go scurrying, but this didn't feel unsafe.

"Thank goodness I wore my jacket!" I said to Amber, a reluctant smile in my voice now.

9

WE REACHED THE SUMMIT, and I felt breathless, not because we'd been walking up a hill for about 40 minutes, but because the city lights at night were stunning.

"Woah," I said, my eyes wide as I stood at the end of the path, "I thought this view was spectacular during golden hour, but night time is magic."

"It's so captivating," Amber said, also staring at the city view in front of us as we walked across the clearing to the edge of the summit. It was about a 10m semi-circle, with the bushland down to our suburb on one side, and a small patch of overgrown shrubs on the other that gave way to a cliff that was the edge of the old quarry.

Up here during the day it felt like Brisbane was laid out in front of you - the wide streets lined with telegraph poles and old Queenslanders spread out like a patchwork quilt all the way to the tall skyscrapers of the city. As the days got warmer and the cicadas could be heard singing right through the bush, a carpet of purple appeared lining most of the streets below as the Jacaranda trees came into bloom.

At night it was a whole new experience. Dim house lights poked through dark patches of suburbia that were bordered by long stretches of bright yellow lights over main roads. Small red, green, and occasional amber lights randomly changed at intersections throughout the suburbs. All of that paled in comparison to the bright lights of the city standing tall and shining like a beacon. The yellow outline of the Story Bridge was the perfect finishing touch to the whole scene - like a sign in the night reminding you from a distance that you're in Brisbane.

When my brain finally came down from its overload of the breathtaking view, it immediately reminded me where we stood: at the edge of the summit clearing, the quarry just over the edge of the shrubs. Of course, thanks to the cliff edge, even during the day all you could see was the very far side of the flattened dirt and old work sheds. At night it was just a blanket of black darkness.

Even though there was no way to see over the edge, I knew that the old quarry lake was at the bottom of that sheer drop, just metres away from where we stood right now. It made me feel sick.

Being up here during the day was fine. The old quarry felt normal, but at night it was like I was walking there in the dark all over again.

"I'm so glad we did this," Amber said, her eyes fixed on the city.

"Yea..." I replied, not feeling good about the memories flashing through my mind.

"It's like what you told me you felt that first all-nighter we did. Right now it's like the whole city is asleep and it's just you and I watching over them. Tonight it's our city! We're like crime fighters... or crime causes... who even knows!"

I gave her a little laugh, trying to sound convincing, but not sure I pulled it off.

"Hey," Amber turned and looked at me now, grabbing both my hands, "What's up Josh?"

I could see in the dim moonlight her eyes searching mine, trying to understand this weird, pulled back version of me.

"I dunno, I'm tired I guess," I gave her a weak smile.

"Okay, I believe you, but are you sure it's not something else?" It was clear she was worried about me. It was written all over her face.

"It's just something up here, at night. I don't know it creeps me out," I exhaled, remembering back to the night I asked her out on the swings. She'd told me the full, heart-breaking story of getting peer pressured into drinking. I knew I had to tell her about the quarry, about Sammy, about that horrible night.

I'd also realised earlier that it had to be me, I was so scared that mum was going to tell her the story then I'd have to try to re-explain it all to Amber - what actually happened, why mum has a different version of events and why I hadn't told her myself.

"Okay," Amber said softly, rubbing one of my arms.

"Sammy, my cousin Sammy," I started, then exhaled.

"Oh yeah, that your mum was talking about tonight, it sounds like you guys were close?"

"Do you want to sit down?" I asked Amber, motioning down toward the grass of the clearing.

"Yea, of course," she said, sitting down while still holding my hand. Her tone suggested she knew this was going to be an important story for me to tell.

"Sammy is a year older than us, but I basically grew up with her like she was my sister. Around our house all the time, our families holidayed together basically every school break in primary school. We wrote each other letters during the term and I honestly worshipped her. If Sammy said it I believed it, there was no question, she knew all the things."

Amber was picking blades of grass and playing with them between her fingers, but her eyes and attention were solely on me.

"I remember when she was in grade seven, she was so excited about going to high school the next year, like as if primary school was a cage that was holding her back. I couldn't relate at all. High school seemed terrifying. I think I had American movies in my head and I was expecting to get thrown into my locker and beaten up every lunchtime or something, I dunno." I laughed, Amber smiled and shook her head at me.

"Little Josh sounds like a cutie," she winked.

"Anyway, I admitted to her how scared I was the summer holidays before she started high school, and in my little eleven-year-old brain I thought that this might make her think about how scary high school was going to be and then she'd freak out and we could be scared together!"

"Team work!" Amber laughed.

"Seriously, I could be an inspirational speaker!" I joined her in laughter.

"Anyway, she wasn't scared. She promised me she'd get me all the inside knowledge, share all the tips and tricks with me, tell me all the stories and that kind of settled me down I guess. Pretty much all of grade seven, anytime I was nervous about going to high school next year, I'd just remind myself that Sammy was lining up all the tips and tricks for me!"

"And she did, by the way, she told me I'd be popular at boys schools if you were friends with girls, and assured me that my friendship with her and her friends would be the perfect start. She told me it was a lot like primary school in that there aren't big tough bullies walking around waiting to chuck you in the bin and she told me she could get me alcohol so I'd know how to go to parties."

"Wow, she was getting drunk and supplying alcohol at thirteen that's so young!" Amber's eyes were confused.

"So I guess this is the story I've been wanting to tell you since our first night at the park..." I said, meeting her gaze and feeling ashamed.

Amber looked back with concern in her eyes. In the distance, I could hear a siren breaking through the cold midnight air. I looked up at the bridge. Despite it feeling like the city was asleep, I knew that right now where those buildings stood tall, thousands of people just a few years older than us were partying and getting drunk. I knew that was coming for me, and I had no idea how I was going to cope.

"In the summer holidays between grade seven and grade eight Sammy told me she was going to take me to a party to meet her friends. We had to tell my parents we were going to the movies with some of her guy friends from First Grammar, so I knew some older kids when I started there in a few weeks time. I totally trusted her. I thought this was part of growing up and that my parents would be knowing less and less about my life. Now I realise what a messed up position that was for a twelve-year-old to be in."

"Yea wow, you were just a kid..." Amber said, as if thinking out loud.

"So we walked to the party that Friday night. The whole way there I was asking Sammy questions - asking her who all the people there were and what they'd be talking about, and what time we'd need to leave and if I could just stay by her side. She stopped, grabbed my shoulders, she was chewing gum but I could smell beer on her breath, and she told me to just shut up and chill out, to not be the weird nerdy kid who talked too much. So I did. I shut up, and we walked. Walked there," I said, pointing down over the ridge.

"At the quarry?" Amber asked.

"Yea. I mean, we'd been there so much as kids, exploring with our parents and stuff, so it was kinda cool to go there when it was packed out with older kids. They'd lit a huge bonfire near the lake, and there were eskies and deckchairs all around it. Music was pumping, people were chatting and laughing and shrieking. I remember thinking that this is what a good time sounds like. Probably 50-80 people were there, the girls were almost all in bikinis and the guys almost all shirtless. They all seemed like much older kids, but were probably younger than we are now.

So Sammy introduced me to her friends, girls from school and some guys from First Grammar. They were nice enough, but it was obvious I did not fit in. Then one of the boys handed me a beer. I was so scared, so scared that I'd go to jail, I was scared that I'd hate the taste and vomit or something, but I knew I couldn't turn it down, I knew I wasn't cool enough to be here and I was on thin ice as it was."

"Oh Josh," Amber hugged herself into me.

"I remember how foul it tasted. The first thought I had was to do anything to not give it away with my face. The second thought was utter confusion about why dad and his friends are so keen on drinking beer if it tastes this gross. They picked up that I wasn't liking it while I tried to fake my way through a straight face. Sammy told me to just take big mouthfuls and get buzzed, then it would taste better. So I did, as all the boys she'd introduced me to encouraged me along.

As I finished that beer, one of the boys handed me a Vodka Cruiser, a pink one, making a crack about it being more my style as Sammy and everyone else laughed. He was right though, it was like a creaming soda and I loved it. I started talking with them then and it was easy. I noticed Sammy and some boy slip away together. I kept eyes on them as they headed into the shadows of the cliff."

Amber sat and listened, moving her eyes between the grass that she was plucking and tearing and looking up at me, taking in every word of the story. I told her about how I drank a lot. ot that a twelve-year-old needed to drink much at all before they'd be in trouble, but I would have been barely able to stand up.

I told her about the guys egging me on to swim in the lake, how popular I felt when they all agreed it'd be funny if I did it.

Then I told her about going to find Sammy and tell her I was going for a swim.

When I stumbled over to Sammy, her friends and the guys I'd been hanging out with giggling in the background, she was lying on a rug clearly, I now understand, having sex with some guy who I'm sure goes to my school but I have no recollection of his face.

"She told me to F off." Amber was staring intently at me now, so much sympathy in her eyes I couldn't look at her. I stared out at the city.

"I told her I was going for a swim in the quarry lake, that I didn't care if our parents thought it was dangerous because we're adults. She told me she didn't care and told me again to F off. So I turned around and looked toward the lake. The older guys started egging me on through laughter, chanting my name. I actually remember standing there and thinking that there wasn't any obvious thing that could go wrong, so I ran, stumbling, probably not that fast and I jumped in."

I felt Amber's arm grab mine and tighten.

"Oh no," she said.

"Oh no," I repeated, still staring off toward the city, nodding. The next part of the story I'd never verbalised before, I actually wasn't even sure if I had the words to explain it. I took a deep breath.

"I'm not sure what parts of this I remember, what parts I've made up and what parts were just drunken stupidity, but I remember hitting the water and it actually being quite nice on the hot summer night. It felt a bit thicker than water, but still nice. I started swimming up toward the surface, but it wasn't coming. I was confused about how deep I'd jumped, but I kept going. The surface never came. I freaked out. I couldn't find the surface. I could see light, kind of, but I couldn't work out which direction it was in. I was running out of air and I had no idea what to do. I screamed. I took in water. I could feel myself running out of oxygen. I was thrashing around, trapped. I had nowhere to go. I had nothing. I was going to die and my parents thought I was at the movies."

I paused, realising my breathing was heavy. I'd been talking really fast, and I felt a tear roll down my cheek. Amber pulled herself into my chest again, rubbing my arm.

"Someone dived in and grabbed me, a guy, but not any of the guys I'd met. They sat with me, making sure I caught my breath. I'd tried so hard to be cool, but here I was soaking wet, loudly crying, telling anyone that would listen I needed to go home. Then I vomited. I heard people say ew and laugh. Weirdly, that was the moment I felt the most scared. Suddenly, I realised the compassion and kindness that had surrounded my innocent life until that moment wasn't something I'd always experience.

Anyway, someone found Sammy, and she stormed over to me, yelling about how I'd stuffed up her whole night, grabbed my arm and dragged me away.

On the way home, she just went on and on about how I'd never survive high school and I deserved how those guys treated me and would treat me every day. I thought she'd be so upset when she heard about how I nearly died, but she wouldn't even listen to me, telling me it wasn't that bad and I just needed to grow up."

"She sounds lovely," Amber chimed in.

"Well, that's the thing, until that moment I thought she was the most wonderful human on the entire planet, but hindsight is such a weird thing hey?! Like I look back on conversations we had as we were growing up, particularly in the final years of high school, and I realise she was so scared of not being liked, so insecure about everything, I was probably the one safe place where she felt like she'd be loved no matter what." I'd only realised this over the summer just gone, and I had basically pushed it out of my mind because I didn't know how to deal with it.

"So here's the good part of the story, when we go to your street on the walk home she stopped and said 'here's the deal, you're drunk, and your parents will make sure you and I are grounded for life if you tell them what happened, so I'm going to tell them a story and we just have to stick to it, okay.'"

"Oh gosh..." Amber replied, predicting what would come next.

"She told my parents at the movies I'd shown everyone some alcohol that I'd got hold of and kept asking everyone to drink it with me, they'd all said no, but I drank it with my Coke and then when we were leaving I dived into the fountain at the shopping centre."

"You've told them the truth, right?" Amber asked, looking seriously at me.

"I thought Sammy was right. If I told them the actual story both our lives would be ruined. She'd promised me this story would keep us both safe...I know I was an idiot."

"You were twelve!" Amber angrily interjected. "A kid!"

"Yea, well, anyway, they put me to bed that night. I cried

silently until I passed out, then spent the night dreaming I was drowning. At first my parents didn't really believe the story, but I filled the holes, telling them I just found the alcohol while Andy and I walked up Whites Hill one day."

"Josh... I, I'm so sorry you went through this," Amber sounded breathless, shocked by my story.

"I realise now that I was basically suffering PTSD in the months after. Some nights I couldn't sleep and the nights I did were restless, filled with dreams that I was drowning. But I couldn't tell anyone.

I replied to Sammy's messages the next day. She was excited we got away with the excuse. I didn't know what to say. I wanted to tell her I was scared I was going to die and couldn't sleep, but I thought she'd be mad at me again. Then I just didn't know how to talk to her anymore. Eventually she stopped trying."

———

"Has she ever apologised?" Amber asked.

"I think she's tried, at family Christmas the year before last. She tried to get one on one with me but I kept finding excuses to be too busy. As we left, she mentioned trying to catch up sometime. I politely agreed, then ignored her messages. Last family Christmas, she moved her place next to mine. I told her I didn't feel up to talking with her about anything. She got the message. I blocked her on my phone that afternoon."

"Fair enough." Amber nodded her head, deep in thought.

"And not because I'm like trying to tell her she's dead to me. I just don't want the dreams and the anxiety and the trapped feelings to return and I think talking to her might bring them, you know?"

"Josh, you don't need to justify any of this to me, or anyone. I feel like my heart is breaking imagining twelve-year-old you going through this." As Amber spoke I exhaled, feeling a weight I didn't even know I was carrying lift off my shoulders.

"Are you okay with questions?" Amber's eyes looked into mine, filled with sympathy.

"Of course, of course," I said, trying to lift the mood a little, putting forward a smile that we both knew was hiding tears.

"Why haven't you told your parents?"

"Well, after all was said and done, it was kind of like forgive and forget - and they have, like I can tell, they 100% trust me. So they never bring it up, or hold it against me or anything, so I've just let sleeping dogs lie, if that makes sense."

Amber paused, picked a blade of grass and looked at it against the view in front of us.

"I just think..." she started, staring silently at the blade of grass before gently discarding it beside her and looking up at me.

"I think about the way your mum was talking about you and Sammy tonight. I'm sure she trusts you and all, but it feels to me like she'd want to know the truth of what happened. I mean, I'd be confused if I heard the fake story. It's not who you are. Or maybe you were when you were twelve, but I don't think so," Amber said with a light smile that suggested a twelve-year-old party animal was too cool for the fifteen-year-old sitting before her.

"I guess I haven't thought about what they think of it all now. I just assumed that like me, they were glad that we didn't have to think about it and that it was in the past.

Sometimes mum will have a moment, or shoot dad a look that makes me think she's still waiting for another night like that to happen, but, yea, I don't know. I don't think about it much."

Amber snuggled into me. We sat there staring at the view ahead of us. The distant sound of a loud car or far-off siren occasionally joined with the dull hum of the city at night. Then I felt it: just us, watching over the city; in our own little bubble; no one else in the world was part of this magical moment.

"You're better than living life hiding behind your mistakes," Amber told me.

10

"CAL, CAL, CAL! I may have just seen the CHEESIEST thing of my LIFE" Andy yelled through laughter. He stood in the middle of my room, Facetiming his girlfriend, "Josh and Amber have flashlights that they shine onto the trees they can see from each other's bedrooms to say I love you before they go to bed at night!" He burst into laughter on the last word. I tried to glare at him, but I have to admit if it was him and Cal, I'd be laughing too.

"Oh my gosh! Let them be romantic, you ass!" She laughed back to him.

"You LITERALLY sent me a picture of Amber sneakily writing a letter to Josh during a maths class with the caption 'VOMIT CITY,' don't take the high ground now Callista" Andy replied, both of them bursting into fits of laughter.

After their phone call had finished, Andy lay on the mattress in the centre of my room, me up on my bed as I explained to him where the torch flashing came from.

"It actually only started two weeks ago, to be honest," I

told him. "Last week of the June school holidays. We'd been sneaking out to our quarry lookout spot every night."

"Wait, what?!" He asked. "You guys were sneaking out on the holidays?"

I nodded to him, trying to pretend I didn't also think this was totally badass.

"I don't know how to categorise you," Andy looked at me confused, "you won't go to parties cause you're too much of a goody-goody, but you sneak out at night to smooch your girlfriend?"

"I told you, people at parties are weird and do weird things, but can I finish my story PLEASE?" I faked frustration at him. "So it was freezing cold, we were getting heaps of jackets on, climbing the hill and lying under the stars watching movies on her laptop."

"Oh that's like romantic movie level! My boy knows how to get laid! I bet you let her stare up at the stars while you..."

"Come on man!" I interrupted him. "The stars are magical from up there by the way, it's really cool."

"Dude, you're not turning me on, what's this got to do with your light show?"

"Well, it was halfway through holidays and we were about to head up. I was crouched in the bushes at the back of her garden.... And no that was not a euphemism," I quickly said before he could interrupt me. "She jumped out of her laundry window as usual and starts making her way up the backyard, when boom her back door opens and her dad is standing there with the brightest torch of all time. I'd already stood up, we were both caught."

"Ohhhhhhh bro" Andy whispered, clearly disappointed for me.

"I was sent home. The next morning mum woke me up FUMING and our parents worked together to ensure we never snuck out again - basically messaging each other anytime something suss happened, like putting deodorant on before bed."

"How badly did you cop it from your parents?" He asked.

"They were mad, but they got over it by the afternoon. The worst was when I next visited Amber and her dad gave me this lecture on how he trusts me with Amber but how right now he's the man in her life that has to take care of her. And how I'm not ready for the responsibility of looking after her, and how he doesn't ever want to feel let down by me like that with his daughter again."

"That's deep!" Andy said, feeling my pain.

"Yea, the stabbing part was when he was like 'you know Josh, I never feel worried about my girl dating you. Last night was the first time I ever had to feel unhappy about her boyfriend choice. Don't let it happen again.'" Even saying that made me feel so guilty and vulnerable.

"That sucks man, that really sucks."

We lay in silence for a bit.

"So anyway, we'd say goodnight to each other on the phone each night after that, and one night I had my torch and shone it up on the tree and asked if she could see it. It kinda became our thing. Caught by the torch, now we use the torch to stay together." I winked at Andy, he rolled his eyes back.

"You reckon you and Amber will ever come partying?" Andy asked me after a minute or two.

"I dunno man, it just all seems so weird. Like I don't know what people will say or do, or if I'll do something stupid or someone will do something to make me look dumb." I couldn't find the right words to say. My mind was spinning. Surely this was the moment I should tell my best mate about what happened down at the quarry. The story I'd been suppressing and pretending didn't exist for the last four years of our friendship.

"That's why you get drunk! So you don't care! And you do the weird stuff too!" He replied with a tone that suggested he really believed he'd solved that problem.

"No way," I laughed, my face was burning as I continued pretending I didn't have a near-death experience following that exact advice. "I am so not prepared for what I'd do drunk, or what people would say about me. No chance."

"Well no pressure," he said genuinely, "but I'd like you around when I'm making a fool of myself at parties"

"Thanks man," I replied, "I think Amber wants to go to the afterparty for the combined colleges music night."

"Awwww hell yea, I'll be there!" Andy sat up to hi-five me, "It'll actually be the maddest first party for you guys - tame, but also the possibility that everything will hit the fan. Know what I mean?"

"I wasn't planning on joining her!" I sternly told him "It actually makes me feel sick about her being there though, like... I mean, I don't know, but what if someone does something stupid and hurts her or... worse."

"Dude, stop overthinking it....and come so none of that can happen!" He said with a cheeky, victorious grin.

Talk of the afterparty was probably the hardest situation I'd dealt with in Amber and my relationship. I didn't want to be some controlling loser and tell her she couldn't go, or worse be all passive aggressive about it so that she felt guilty about going.

On the other hand though, I was so scared. Scared she'd enter that world that had scarred me for life and I had no plan of ever going back to, but she'd love it, and it would force a wedge between us.

11

"YOU'RE ACTUALLY SUCH A DOUCHEBAG!" Amber yelled at me, launching herself across the room ready to slap my face.

"I did that five minutes ago! How did you JUST REALISE?!" I put my arms out to defend myself from her, giggling at how pretty she still looked despite the chocolate now dripping from her hair down her face.

"Do you know how long it will take to wash CHOCO-LATE out of my hair!" She cried, trying not to laugh.

"Hey! You said I was being boring following the recipe and that I needed to learn to experiment," I said, laughing at myself.

"WITH THE MUFFINS!!! NOT WITH MY HAIR!!!"

"Ohhhhh, well you should have made that clearer. Here, let me fix it." I said, leaning down to kiss her on her choco-late smudged forehead.

"I just melt every time you kiss me on the forehead" she sighed. I knew her beautiful eyes would be looking up at me in the cutest possible way right now, but this gag wasn't done. I turned the gentle kiss into a lick, right up the choco-late path.

"EWWW!!! YOU'RE SO GROSS!!!!" She squealed, pulling away from me.

Amber's parents were at her uncle's 50th, so we had basically all afternoon and night to hang out at her place - with the promise to her parents that no sneaking out would happen. I had a plan to make tonight fun and romantic - to go bigger than the night I asked her out. It started with baking muffins, cookies...anything with sugar ahead of our movie night.

I was trying to work out the right moment to bring up the afterparty next week. Stressing about it was taking up way too much of my brain, and honestly, I almost felt silly that I wasn't telling Amber. We shared every little thing with each other, surely we could share this without me making her do something she didn't want to do?

I was also aware that this week had been hard for Amber. Lauren, her best friend since they were in kindy, was being a real cow to her. Three afternoons this week she'd arrived at my house all cheery, her hair in a high ponytail, wearing bright pink activewear and a giant smile on her face, ready for our afternoon walk, and the moment we were in the park and away from houses her face would crinkle and she'd burst into tears.

Lauren had taken to pointing out every calorie that Amber ate, and asking passive aggressive questions like "Are you going to eat ALL that?"

Anytime the Combined Colleges Music Performance came up Lauren would make comments about how Amber was only invited to be in the main band because she helped the music teachers clean up the room after rehearsal and they felt like they owed her the favour.

This was totally incorrect. I thought Amber was beautiful all the time, but when she sat down in front of her piano it's like she was elevated to superhero. She was so talented. So fantastic. Just perfect. She'd make the tiniest of mistakes (apparently) but I would have no idea, except when she'd point it out and explain it, and even how she explained it was magical, like a language I'd never heard before.

Amber, being Amber, refused to let this rut with Lauren go untouched. On our Thursday afternoon walk she mapped out a plan to have an open conversation with Lauren. She was worried that she'd upset her, or was in some other way at fault.

Then, Friday afternoon we were sitting at the top of the hill, Amber's head tucked deep into my chest as she heaved heavy tears. When she pulled Lauren aside at their lockers at lunch, Lauren very loudly yelled "Why do you make EVERYTHING a drama Amber? Why can't you just grow up like the rest of us are instead of being a little baby crying all day?"

Cal and Amber's other friends comforted her and told her Lauren had been being especially weird to her all week, but it didn't help. She felt like the whole grade was laughing at her and that she'd need to lay low.

Seeing Amber upset was difficult. I wished I had the words that could make her pain and anxiety go away. All I could do was tell her it was horrible and hug her while she talked. I wanted to message Lauren and tell her how much she was hurting Amber. But Amber told me that would make it worse.

I started flicking through Lauren's Instagram photos and impersonating her in each one with the bitchiest voice I could. Amber laughed, and smiled and it made me happy that her world was just a little bit better.

. . .

As our muffins cooled down on the bench, the sweet smell of sugar and chocolate filled the kitchen air and begged me to partake of their choc-chip goodness. I'd already tried to eat one, against Amber's advice, gobbling the fresh-out-of-the-oven muffin down and immediately regretting my decision as it burnt my tongue. Amber's laughter could probably be heard from ten streets away as I rushed to spit it in the bin.

"It's 6pm, time for YOU to go pick the pizza up!" I told Amber as I grabbed her hand and spun her around like we were dancing.

"I am not your slave, boy!" She countered me, with a total girl boss look on her face.

"I know, and trust me, I'd love to walk down with you, but I have work to complete here for at-home date night!" I said as I pulled her in and kissed her forehead.

"Don't you DARE exploit cute forehead kisses to get what you want!" she said, glaring up at me with the cutest puppy dog eyes before she grabbed her phone and walked off with a mischievous smile. "It better be good" she said as she walked out the door.

The Domino's pizza was down next to the supermarket, about two blocks from Amber's. I estimated I had about 15 minutes to get this sorted out before she returned.

I grabbed the huge pile of pillows and her blanket off her bed and headed for the living room. I put the pillows on the floor, then grabbed rope from my bag, hanging it from the blinds above the balcony door and the window across the room, then hung a sheet over the top. The perfect pillow fort with prime TV viewing access. Battery operated fairy lights completed the look inside.

"Honey, I'm home!" Amber sung from the front door.

I walked over to the top of the staircase, looking down on her

"Oh Romeo, Romeo where for art thou?" I replied.

"I'm clearly here, dammit Juliet you need to get your eyes tested!" She smirked back.

"Wow, that's a beautiful sight..." I said looking down at her, then just as an uncontrollable smile broke on her face I added, "just a shame you're in my view, ruining the beautiful pizza."

When Amber got to the top of their stairs even my insult from before couldn't keep the smile off her face.

"Oh baby, I love it!" She cheered, jumping into the fort with our pizza and garlic bread, "Get in here and KISS ME!" she cried.

I dived in after her, grabbing her around the waist and pulling her into me. I kissed her lightly, our eyes closed, holding each other. My arm pulled her tighter and she lightly bit my top lip. The air was electric as we held on to each other, our mouths still together.

Amber pulled away, just an inch from my face, our eyes locked to one another.

"I'm so lucky," she said.

"It scares me the day you realise that isn't true," I told her.

"Never!" she laughed.

We ate pizza, spooning each other as we watched a DVD copy of "10 Things I Hate About You".

Sheltered under the twinkling canopy of fairy lights in our little fort we were back in our own world. A moment of magic was happening and nobody else knew about it. We lay there together watching the movie, our conversations ebbing and flowing effortlessly - peppered with "This or That" questions whenever the conversation reached a natural lull. "Pizza or fries?"

"Pizza for sure"

"Okay, sand or water?"

"Holy moly, always water, I actually hate going to the beach because sand is the WORST! It gets everywhere, is impossible to clean off, so then it's in your thongs, your togs, your shower!" I told her, pulling myself up to my knees for full dramatic effect.

"Wait... what?! You don't like the beach?" She asked, shocked.

"Okay, I love the beach, but I hate sand, therefore I end up avoiding the beach to avoid the sand."

"Wow, I never thought I'd date a psychopath... but now we need to break up" she said, rolling her eyes and pretending to delete my contact off her phone.

"YOU CAN'T BREAK UP WITH ME, YOU'RE FIRED" I said, falling into her.

As I lay on her lap in our cosy little cubby, the TV playing the trailer of some corny sounding romcom in the background, butterflies filled my stomach. Despite how perfect tonight had been, I knew that at some point I was going to have to tell Amber that I couldn't do a party, and that I was really anxious about her going to the afterparty.

I started to count down from ten in my head, working up the courage to start the conversation.

"What are you deep in thought about?" Amber asked me, looking back from her position as little spoon.

"I can't stop worrying about the party next weekend" I admitted, breathing out a heavy sigh.

"Let's go up to the quarry!" She replied, her eyes lit up.

It's not like she was ignoring me, more like she thought this was an appropriate response to what I'd just said.

"Wait, what? No, your dad will kill us." I replied, kind of annoyed that it took me so much vulnerability to admit this thing I've been worried sick about and she just ignored me.

"You have to trust me," Amber looked me straight in the eyes, holding both my hands, "lets go to the quarry, you just have to trust me on this."

"I don't think we can. I can't let your dad down like that again, he'll think I'm a douche! I can't even think about how he'll look at me," I felt like I wanted to vomit.

"Josh," she pulled me close and looked straight into my eyes, "he's all bark no bite! But we won't get caught, trust me, okay?"

12

———

THE WALK through the bushland was freezing. When we reached the summit, Amber and I lay together on a blanket on the ground, an icy wind sweeping past intermittently and forcing us to snuggle into each other.

"There used to be a house up here," I broke the silence, wanting to get the conversation started.

"Really?" Amber asked, her tone questioning if I was making this up.

"Yea, for real! In fact, there's part of the concrete foundations just over that way." I pointed to the far end of the clearing.

"There actually is! I've seen it before, but I just figured it was like a lookout from the war or something!"

"Nah, the White family built a house up here. They had a road that came up where the quarry is now and everything. The city council were desperate to get the place back, so after he died they did everything to get hold of the estate."

"Because of the view and the bush?"

"It's actually so much better than that! The family started serving food up here, then illegally started selling alcohol and hosting parties and just trashing the area. The city council didn't want anyone else to have the opportunity to keep that going."

"He's like Brisbane's Gatsby!"

"Oh, my gosh! I never even considered this!"

"Maybe we need to set up a green light here..."

"I really vibe with it, though. I've always wanted a house that's like an open door policy. Just people coming and hanging out there whenever, hosting big dinners and get-togethers. A place where people just always feel welcome and want to go."

"I think I'd love that..." Amber replied as if she was coming out of a deep thought. "We need to buy this place back!" Amber continued, suddenly sitting up, her eyes excited and wide open.

"This could be our place! We'd host massive dinners up on the hill with party lights in the trees and basically everyone in Brisbane can see it and wants to come find it!" Even as I said this, I was aware of the quarry and its horrible history lurking just over the edge of where we sat. But as Amber and I made more plans for a life together - a life that sounded like my wildest dreams come true - I just had to believe that the quarry and all the pain that it held would one day be in the past.

"It's going on the bucket list!" Amber noted the plan on her phone.

"I love us," I said, smiling again at the stars.

"We're pretty awesome..." Amber said as we snuggled back into each other. The tip of my nose felt so cold that it might fall off, but I couldn't think of anywhere else I'd rather be at this moment.

"Remember the first night we snuck out?" Amber eventually said, breaking the silence, "I'd done nothing like that before, until that moment my parents pretty much knew where I was and who I was with every second of every day."

"That was such a good night," I said, smiling to myself.

"The stars were like they are tonight," Amber was looking straight up at the sky. With our eyes adjusted to being outside, the bright clusters of stars forming galaxies shone so brightly above us.

"That night I felt the wildest I think I'd ever felt in my life, and I thought it must just be so normal for you to sneak out and break rules like that."

"I am a bad boy," I replied, putting on my attempt at a tough guy tone.

"You are SO NOT a bad boy!" Amber was half laughing, "If I'm honest, I actually thought the thing that would break us up was going to be how much of a rule breaker you were! I thought sneaking out was just something you did all the time. I actually lay in bed one night in those early days working out what you might be involved with that would become the line I'd draw and have to dump you. But the more I got to know you the more I saw that us sneaking out wasn't a bad boy move. It was someone who loves fun and adventure and being around people he loves."

Butterflies fluttered all through my stomach, causing me to feel tingly all over, and I'm sure if I tried to talk right now I would cry. I would never have described myself like that, never even thought it. But sometimes it takes a person who really listens to you, watches you, someone who really loves you to show you the best of who you are.

"And that's what used to confuse me, and now just breaks my heart about you and parties. Please don't think I'm downplaying what happened to you at the quarry, because it was horrible and you have a right to be scarred by that night, but it's stolen so much from you and that sucks, Josh!

It's so obvious you want to expand your friendships and be part of fun, exciting things. Like seriously, nobody's brain goes to doing things the fun way as quickly as yours. Look at what you did at my place tonight!

I think the whole party thing would be the most natural place for you to be you, and be, literally, the life of the party."

She was right, at least I think she was right, I didn't disagree with anything she said. Those descriptions all lined up with things that intrigued and excited me. But I just imagined living them out when I was older and in environments more controlled than a backyard full of unpredictable teenagers drinking alcohol.

"But because of everything..." Amber continued right when I thought it was my time to talk. My body tensed, surprised and maybe a little bit nervous about what she'd say next.

"I think," she hesitated, "I think you have so much trust in the people around you, and you're so loyal to them, but for anyone outside that circle you're just so skeptical of them. You're so afraid they'll hurt you or embarrass you or... or let you down like Sammy and her friends did. That night has meant that you put so much work into making sure you have control of how everything will go. It's not like you're controlling, and please don't get me wrong you are not controlling or anything like that..."

"Amber, it's okay" I stopped her. I could tell she was scared she'd upset me and was talking faster and faster. "I love you."

"Okay, but you can tell me if that was mean or if I'm wrong. I could be wrong like I'm not a psychologist or anything..."

"You're not wrong," I pulled her close to me. "I just didn't think about any of that till now..."

"When we ran into Matt at bowling, you were just so anxious and I didn't understand what had happened, but when I was thinking about all of this, it was so obvious. Josh, you need to know that what happened that night down there at the quarry. That's not a normal thing. That will not be something that happens with me, or Andy, or Cal. Even if people you don't trust are involved, most people would never consider treating someone like that as acceptable."

I exhaled deeply, then Amber looked up at me, my arms tightly wrapped around her, my heart beating so fast.

"You're a really great person to be around, Josh, and it breaks my heart that night all those years ago has taken the best bits of you away from so many people. I'd do almost anything to break you out of it and see there's people just waiting to get the awesome experience that is adventuring with Josh."

I hugged her tighter. My brain was running at a million miles an hour, but I had no idea what I was thinking.

"Maybe it's not just the fear of... well, ending up drowning again. I'm also so afraid of letting everyone down again," I said slowly, both to myself and Amber. She looked back up at me.

"You mean your parents?"

"Yea my parents, but as messed up as this is, the most vivid memory I have from that night is when I went over to Sammy when she was hooking up with that guy, she looked so disappointed in me that I'd ruined her night. All my life up until then I thought she was always by my side, my number one, but in that moment I'd disappointed her so much she didn't even care if I got hurt."

"Oh Josh, you're so much better than having to feel like this," Amber leaned up and kissed me on the chin.

"Perhaps this isn't my place to say, but I think you're holding on more tightly to your fears from that night than any of it's holding on to you..." Amber let that idea hang in the air.

"You're okay Josh. Your parents love you so much, you have amazing friends and you're safe. In fact, you're more than okay, you're more than safe. You're thriving."

"It really is holding on to me." I took a deep breath in.

Amber's warm, rugged up body was softly fitting into mine. I could feel her gently breathing as her head lay tucked into my chest, her hand stroking mine. I didn't know how to process any of this conversation, but the fact that Amber had talked it all out with me and hadn't thought I was an idiot for going along with Sammy's plan that night made me feel the most okay with it all than I'd been in four years. I didn't want to move. I never wanted this moment to end.

"I've never felt this close to somebody in my life..." I whispered.

"I felt that the first night we hung out; like I'd found my soulmate. But I'd never admit it because teenagers who think they're soulmates are lame. If this isn't actual love... I don't know if I'd be able to mentally cope with how great it must be."

"Don't worry, I already think you're really lame," I told Amber as I tickled her sides. She shrieked with laughter and looked up at me. As soon as I stopped she gave me a death stare. I leaned down and kissed her gently.

Amber snaked her hand behind my neck, pulling me down to her mouth and kissing me deeply. My arm wrapped around her tightly, our bodies shifting to be side by side, my other hand gently pulling her hair as our breathing got heavier - desperate and hungry for more of each other.

I pulled her tighter again, and she wrapped one leg over me.

We'd been passionate before, but this felt different. I was

just so desperate to share the deeper emotional connection I'd felt with her tonight. I needed to be closer to her.

Her cold hand dipped under my shirt, eagerly exploring every inch of my back and pulling me closer to her.

I grabbed her hair again, my hand moving its way to her hip and then slowly under her jumper.

I pulled my mouth slightly away from hers. "I don't know what this feeling is," I said between heavy breaths, "but I feel like I'm going to explode if I'm not closer to you!"

"Same," she replied panting, her eyes glued to mine. She went back in for a kiss, softly biting my bottom lip. She held it there for a second and I saw her eyes considering something. Then all at once she closed her eyes and wrapped an arm around my neck, pulling me closer as she kissed me deeply and pushed her hips into mine.

The feeling was amazing. I pushed back and her kissing became more feverish and desperate.

Back and forth slowly, we worked into each other. Then suddenly she pushed back.

"Wait!" she panted, holding a hand up and catching her breath. "I'm not done being serious yet!"

I lay on my side staring at her, stunned. I had never felt like this before and my body was screaming at me that we should not stop here!

"Okay," I breathlessly replied.

"People love you, and you love people, and I just think everyone's losing because of a really messed up situation that happened to you - that you had NO control over. I know you want to have this exact opposite conversation with me, but I think you need to come next Saturday. You'll be surrounded by people who you love and trust and deserve your trust. I think you'll realise that the experience you have of parties and drinking is not accurate at all.

You had one terrible, messed up night that you absolutely deserve to be wounded by, but it's painted a picture of parties and people that's stealing so much of who you are."

"Okay," I repeated with my head still spinning and no ability to even think about what she'd just said.

She let out a little laugh, "And no, I'm not trying to use sex to get what I want. Just think about it and let's talk some more in a few days..."

"Uhmmm, Amber, you know that wasn't sex right..." I teased her, trying really hard not to give away how much my head was still spinning.

She smiled at me, her arms finding their way back around me, "shut up and lets get back to where we were," she said, going in for a deep kiss and wrapping her legs around mine.

13

———

"COULD we please have a moment of silence," Andy turned to us the moment we'd jumped out of his mum's 4WD, slinging his backpack, stuffed with his jumper and as many cans of Bundy Rum as the remaining space would allow, over his shoulder.

"Josh and Amber, you've made it. I'll be honest, I thought you'd always be lame, but today you've proved me wrong. You've shown me you're slightly less lame and will party with me." He held a solum face through this, then suddenly looked up, pointing down the side of the house we'd arrived at. The sound of loud teenagers and something from The Killers was in the air. "Now let's go!"

Andy and Cal started marching down the small dirt path past the wooden Queenslander. A slightly overgrown hedge covering the fence forced us into single file. The smell of sausages and onion cooking on a BBQ made my stomach rumble, reminding me I hadn't had dinner yet. Distant voices, occasional loud laughs, and screams rang out. Amber grabbed my hand and walked just in front of me.

"This'll be fun, I promise," she said, turning over her shoulder with an excited smile.

"I'm feeling it," I said, smiling back. And I was.

It was weird to think that only an hour ago I'd been sitting next to her parents, watching her deep in composed concentration behind a black grand piano on Cavendish College's theatre stage. A blue ribbon neatly in her hair. She was gently leaning forward as she sung into the microphone. Amber's singing voice was effortlessly beautiful, and despite there being 500 people sitting around me, I was captivated - totally in awe of how everything that seemed to come out of my girlfriend was magical.

Even now as she walked in front of me - a little skip in her step, wearing a light grey hoody and jeans, her hair still up in a ponytail but the blue private school girl ribbon gone - she shone out all of those things, with added fun and a naïve excitement that suggested adventure was beckoning. I was so proud to be seen with Amber.

We rounded the corner into the backyard, flood lights lit the whole place up. Coloured party lights had been hung between an old swing set and a tree. The yard was littered with classmates of mine and girls from Amber's school. Some were gathered around a fireplace on camping chairs, logs and milk crates.

Another group were sitting in the shadows of the trees and four girls that Amber said caused the bulk of problems in their grade (while also regularly telling everyone how much they hate drama), had clearly already had more than a few drinks as they fell on each other while crawling around the trampoline.

Over at the BBQ stood the unannounced kings of the party. Despite it being July and freezing, all six of the boys were wearing short rugby shorts and thongs. Four of them had already lost their shirts. They were the footy boys by stereotype, but other than finding any excuse to get their shirts off when girls were around, I actually quite liked the "cool group" of our grade.

They were all nice enough to be around, didn't pick on people unnecessarily, but you had to be aware of the chance you'd be pranked whenever you were in their presence. Even as I stood there scoping out the party, the tongs being used to turn our sausages were quietly being edged toward an unexacting Pat Mulcay's penis while he stood there chatting up some girls.

"I'm really vibing this!" I said, turning to Amber with a huge grin, "I think you might have been right, this really could be my kinda place!"

Amber grabbed my hands and quickly stepped on her toes, giving me a peck on the lips.

"I'm glad! Me too!"

For some weird reason, I'd felt so uncomfortable walking into the backyard, like everyone might look up at me with disgust, questioning why I'd shown up. A repeat situation from years ago. An instant recognition that I didn't belong, followed by finding the quickest way to turn me into entertainment and get me out of there. I feared I'd try to talk to people and be met with that look Sammy gave me.

But that fear slipped away like it was never there.

"ARE YOU ABSOLUTELY KIDDING ME" a yelp pierced the air, followed by laughs and yells from the BBQ. Pat's sausage had been grabbed.

———

"Quick, you need this," Andy said, while trying to discreetly shove a can of rum into my hand. My stomach instantly sank.

"I don't think I do," I replied, not engaging with him, instead continuing to take in the party around me.

"QUICK," he insisted, a look of urgency in his eyes, "just take it."

I took it from his hand, more to make this moment end before it became a thing.

"Bro I dunno if you should freak out about this, everyone here is underage and drinking."

"Even so, me giving it to you is supply and I'll get a huge fine," he replied, deadly serious.

I would not drink it.

Just the thought of it made me feel tight in the chest. All the horrible anxiety of that night in the lake came rushing in and suddenly it was like I wasn't here. Like the party just existed on screens around me. I turned to look at Amber for some kind of grounding. Her face was always a safe place. She had also been given a can, an orange UDL. She had an unsure look in her eye as she faced me, but lightly shrugged, mouthing, "we're okay, you're safe," as she opened it.

The tightness in my chest and dissociation with being at the party mostly eased, only slightly lingering in the back of my mind.

But I believed Amber. She was right, she wouldn't let that night happen again. We were safe.

We sat on an old couch under a tarp that had been secured with ropes to the house and trees. A group of Amber and Cal's friends were sitting on the rug in front of us.

I cracked open the can, lifted it to my nose and instantly knew I'd hate the taste of it.

"This smells like ink!" I loudly declared at Andy, bringing my usual dynamic around friends back into order.

One girl looked up. "Oh man, have you never had rum before?"

"Oh man, it is the WORST!" Yelled Bella, apparently already quite a few drinks in. She stumbled over to hug Amber and I.

I put it to my mouth, took a tiny tiny mouthful. It tasted EXACTLY how it smelt, like I'd emptied a pen's ink into my mouth. My face scrunched up.

"Seriously, at Becky Sam's party, I drank nothing but rum all night and woke up in the morning covered in crap…" Bella announced with a tone of warning to the group. Everyone looked at her confused.

"Wait, wait, wait! Do you mean like you'd dropped stuff on yourself and didn't realise till the morning or you poo'd the bed in your sleep?!" I asked, leaning forward.

"I literally did a poo while I slept because of rum," she spelt out, leaning toward me. The group collectively eww'd and laughed at her.

Music pumped, the conversation got louder and funnier and I was drinking alcohol and felt totally in control and safe with Amber by my side. Maybe Amber was right, and I was holding on far more tightly to my fears from that night than they were holding on to me.

Pat wandered over with a sausage hanging down from his pants as the footy boys offered us sausages and bread. At first I was nervous that we were about to become the butt of the joke, but as the girls rolled their eyes, Andy and I laughed harder at each face the sausage accidentally brushed past. Then Bella pulled it out, and he ran away screaming in fake pain.

I slowly sipped away one can of rum, followed by another. Amber, on the other hand, cleared four UDLs in the first hour we were there. Her tongue was a deep purple, and she smelt like lollies.

Lauren was also at the party, but was sitting with another group of people, occasionally looking up at us. Amber was trying to hide the nervous glances she was throwing in Lauren's direction. She was present and having a good night with us, but I could tell the hurt Lauren was causing her was front of her mind.

Eventually Bella blurted out that Lauren kept texting girls to leave our group and chat with her.

I felt Amber tense up. But other than alternating trips to the bathroom, our little group stayed around the couch, chatting to friends as they walked by, or as a slightly tipsy and loudly confident me called them over.

Bella and I had argued over who should sing the male part in the Elephant Love Melody from Moulin Rouge when Amber leaned up to me and said in a shaky voice she was going to the bathroom. I grabbed her arm as she stood up to ask if she was okay. She sounded upset, but there was also something shaken in her tone, maybe fear.

"I just need fresh air," she said, smiling at me. I gently squeezed her hand and watched her walk off, picking up pace as she went and almost tripping a couple of times.

"Is she okay?" Bella asked.

"Yea, I think so... I'm just going to text her though," I replied while tapping away at my phone.

"You two are made for each other," Bella told me, genuinely, even though clearly tipsy.

"Thanks," I replied with a small, dismissive laugh.

"Nah, really," Bella continued, "the way she talks about you guys, you can tell that she's just so happy with how great things are with you guys, like... wait I don't know how to say this." Bella held her hand up at my face, her head slightly cocked as she tried to process something.

"I just think for Amber it's like she's got her family and she's got school and she's got you, like you know that's her stables in life, her like." Her hands began gesturing up and down.

"Her pillars?" I asked, putting on a front of uncertainty and amusement, but inside feeling fireworks of joy going off. I couldn't believe that Amber's friends could see this.

"PILLAR!" Bella clicked at me, "exactly! You're a pillar holding the beautiful roof that is Amber."

I had always thought that drunk people at parties would be unpredictable, weird, angry, violent... scary things. The people here were none of those. People were louder, there was a lot of lying on each other and hooking up, a few sneaking off to secluded places and the occasional girl reappearing from the bushes loudly telling her friends she couldn't believe who she'd hooked up with... whoever the poor fella still hiding in the bushes was.

But it wasn't scary or dangerous.

"Here's the beautiful roof now!" Bella announced toward Amber, who was ambling back over to us, giving a brief smile with a cup of water in hand.

"You okay?" I asked as she sat back down next to me, leaning on my shoulder.

"Yea," she said, looking at her cup and sipping, "I think I might have drunk too much too fast. Everything was spinning and, like my tongue felt numb and I thought I was going to vomit. But Matt grabbed me some water and brought it to me."

"MATT'S HERE!" Bella exclaimed, then stood up, fell back down halfway, Amber and I reached out to help her,

"I've gotta go see Matt and tell him he can blow a trumpet better than anyone I know!" She swayed from side to side as she walked toward the house, stopping to talk to the people around the fire. Then sitting down.

"I think she's forgotten about Matt..." I said, trying to push the idea of Matt attempting to be Amber's hero out of my mind.

"Thanks for letting me peer pressure you into coming," Amber said, taking a big gulp and wincing, "Oh man, even this water tastes weird. I think we were right in choosing not to drink."

We laughed, and I leant down and kissed her on the nose, pulling her into me.

"I'm glad I'm here," I replied, resting my chin on her head, "I'm glad you know me this well."

"Josh, GET YOUR ARSE OVER HERE" I was startled as Pat yelled at me from across the backyard. He was now only wearing undies and his chest was puffed up. Amber looked up at me, confusion in her eyes. I'm sure I looked straight back at her with a slightly more worried look.

"WE ARE PLAYING BEER PONG AND I WILL NOT PLAY UNTIL YOU ARE MY TEAM MATE, YOU GET OVER HERE OR YOU RUIN EVERYONE'S NIGHT. UNDERSTAND?"

"Just sip the beer, maybe?" Amber looked at me with a cheeky grin.

"No, you're clearly unwell. I'm not going to trot off..." I began sternly telling her,

"NO! I'm not dying, I'm right here, my friends are here, you can go do something fun for ten minutes Josh!" she replied, then sipped from her cup and gave me a smile.

14

MINUTES AFTER HAVING a beer thrust in my hand, Beer Pong was underway. I realised pretty fast that I was nowhere near as drunk as everyone else, and it meant I was the only person landing ball after ball in the cups.

After we took out our first opponents, Andy and Cal jumped down the other end of the table. Andy, knowing how competitive I was, picked up that I'd do anything I could to stay sober and keep winning.

"Finish that cup!" Andy yelled. "Right now, make this an even fight and prove you're actually better than everyone!"

I looked over at Amber. Bella had joined her on the couch and was telling her some drunkenly exaggerated story which Amber was attentively tuned into, sitting forward, and maybe looking only a little sick.

I picked up the cup of beer. One of the boys ran over and filled it right to the top then slapped me on the butt.

"For you," I said, holding it up to Andy.

A loud cheer went up as I tried to quickly swallow the drink. It tasted bitter and old. This was basically "the cool group" of our school, and they were here cheering me on. I was one of "the lads." It's not like they'd been horrible to me in the past or anything. We just didn't connect and I figured if I ever entered their world I'd be laughed at.

Then the cup was empty. I slammed it down, and they cheered even louder. My stomach didn't feel great, but I was sure it'd pass. My head was spinning, my eyes watered. I was pumped up.

"LET'S DO THIS!" I yelled, launching the first ball, and almost tripping as I went. It landed in the cup. Well... a cup. Not the one I aimed for, but still a cup.

The competition went on, backward and forward. A lot more drinking from me this time than last time — much bigger gulps, because the crowd demanded it.

We were loud, we were funny. Andy and I weren't the misfits tonight. Everything I feared going to parties would be - this was the exact opposite.

We'd been playing Andy and Cal for eight minutes. The crowd had died down a little and my vision was getting blurry when I felt Amber's hand latch onto my arm.

"Josh," her voice sounded urgent. She looked pale and smelt like vomit.

"What babe?" I asked her, knowing my words were slurring. I tried to concentrate on speaking clearly. I suddenly felt ashamed.

"I just vomited everywhere. I need to go home. Matt's taking me home." Instantly, the joy evaporated, and I felt sick to my stomach. It was stupid that I'd left her when she was sick.

"It's okay, it's okay, I'll call Mum, I know she'll come and pick us up," I said, rubbing her side, aware that everyone was watching on.

"No, no, our parents will hate me. Matt's going to get me home. It's fine, it's fine, you keep playing, I'm sorry I shouldn't have stuffed your game up." She was crying a bit and pushing me toward the table with limp arms.

"Don't be silly, I'm so sorry I left you." She fell into my chest as I said this, hugging me. Matt appeared. He looked at me seriously, not a hint of malice in his eyes. He'd never looked at me like that before. I weakly smiled at him.

"The car's ready," he said. "Did you need to come, Josh? I've only really got room for Amber."

Amber was sick and embarrassed. I knew for sure that our parents would never let us do this again if they saw us like this.

I was scared. So scared of losing Amber. And I was ashamed that I'd gotten drunk and now couldn't get her home. I didn't trust Matt one bit. I didn't care that Amber seemed to think he was nice to her. I'd never seen him be nice to a single person at school without then swinging in to hurt them in some way.

It had happened again. Alcohol had snuck up, tricked me into believing we were all safe and having a good time, then suddenly replaced the moment with something horrific.

I had to shake the thoughts running through my head, the fear and memories from four years ago. In that moment it wasn't about me. Any choice I made other than letting Amber get safely home as soon as possible was selfish.

"How will you get into your house?" I gently asked her.

"I always sneak in when we go on our little walkie walks!" She said, smiling up at me through her tears. I gently pushed one of the vomit crusted strands of hair hanging over her eyes back behind her ear.

"You're sad, vomitty and clearly drunk, but you're still somehow the most perfectly beautiful girl I've ever seen" I told her, and I meant it. I knew the people standing near me were making whipped noises. I knew the drunk crowd were getting rowdier in their demands that the game I was in the middle of kept going, but I didn't care about anything other than making Amber smile again.

"I love you so much" she said, hugged me, kissed me on the chin, then waddled off in Matt's direction.

I felt a hand on my shoulder. Andy had been standing there and I hadn't realised.

"I texted my mum bro," he slurred out, "she's on her way."

Cal came over and hugged me, and we all walked over to the couch and sat down.

Andy was, of course, there for me. We'd partied, we'd had fun, but when it got serious, he was by my side.

I picked up my phone, sent a quick message. I just needed to hear she was going to bed and this whole thing could be a funny joke in the morning.

Josh: Msg me when ur home

It took three attempts to type, and I suddenly understood why Andy's Saturday night texts had become harder to read this year. I put my phone in my pocket.

"What's the deal with Matt, anyway?" Cal asked, loud and slurry "he so clearly wants to get into Amber's pants, but she's so whippppped on you she wouldn't even realise he has a dick!"

I looked up at Cal, wanting to ask her how she knew that, but my head was spinning and Andy was telling her to shut up. Matt was being nice...he wasn't with Amber when she drank too much so it's not like he planned this.

I felt like I was trapped. My chest was tight. I couldn't breathe. It felt like I was in the lake all over again.

15

_____

ANDY'S MUM picked us up in less than ten minutes. Despite the party raging around me, it felt like it took forever for her to get to us.

"Hello guys!" Andy's mum said as we climbed in. She was cheery but there was a slight edge to her tone.

Amber hadn't texted back.

"What's up, mum?" Andy asked, back in party mode.

"You know I hate this," she said, nervously slowing the car as we passed an intersection.

"What?! Josh? Having to be with Josh?? I can stop hanging out with him if you want..." Andy replied, pretending to be serious before looking back at me, smirk on his face, "Sorry bro, my mum says I can't be friends with you anymore... you can get out here..."

"We've had a good run...." I replied, pretending to open the door.

"No, THIS," Andy's mum said, pointing to bright coloured lights approaching fast, silently piercing through the night.

A police car led two ambulances down the road, lights

flashing but sirens off, as if they were trying to respect the quiet of the night.

"I hate being out driving late at night, idiots everywhere!"

I sat staring out the window, gazing at the sleeping homes passing us by. Tonight felt like further proof that drinking and going to parties would never be good news for me. I listened to Amber. I gave them a second chance, and I was right.

Then, I hated myself for being so weird about it. Teenagers get drunk every weekend. This is not some special case where she's suddenly going to die after her first drunken night. Amber would be fine this time tomorrow and she'd want to celebrate the barriers I broke through.

As Andy's mum dropped me off, I hugged Cal, fist pumped Andy and profusely thanked his mum for the late night trip.

Amber still hadn't replied.

I couldn't stop looking at my phone when mum came downstairs to find out how the party was. Then I lay in bed checking any little thing on the internet to burn time, waiting for a reply.

Maybe she's been grounded and isn't allowed her phone anymore.

Maybe she's so drunk she couldn't even use it and just fell straight to sleep.

Maybe she's in hospital getting her stomach pumped.

16

It always feels so weird waking up the second before something happens.

Mum walked into my room as my phone vibrated on the pillow next to me. I must have fallen asleep holding it.

"Sorry," I groggily said to mum assuming she was here to tell me off for waking up so late in the morning.

But it was still dark.

I questioned if I'd slept right through the day.

"My alarm didn't..." I started to say

"Shhh, she said, it's okay, it's early. Come see your dad and I?"

I looked at my phone, 3.19am and two missed calls from Matt.

My stomach sank. I started thinking the worst... was he calling to tell me he'd hooked up with Amber and I needed to stop texting her?

Why had my parents woken me up in the middle of the night? I wondered if they were so mad at me for coming home drunk again they'd decided the anger couldn't wait until morning and dragged me out of bed to talk about it in the middle of the night.

Mum's eyes were bloodshot, like she'd been crying, and dad looked almost empty of emotion as he tapped the seat next to him at the kitchen table.

My mouth was so dry.

"Can I get water?" I asked.

"Your mum will get one for you mate," dad replied. His tone was friendly, which surprised me.

I sat down. Dad exhaled and mum brought me my cup of water, putting a hand on my back as she sat down.

"I've just got off the phone to Amber's dad, buddy" dad told me. I looked up, shock in my eyes. Were they really coordinating our punishment in the middle of the night?

"Look, it was our first party. We didn't know how much alcohol we were having..." I felt mum's hand tense on my back.

"Mate... no, Josh mate. Amber's been involved in an accident."

"Oh no, Oh no... I shouldn't have let her go, is she at home? Can I go see her? Is she okay?"

Mum took in a quivered breath next to me.

"Mum?" I said, my voice going higher like a little boy afraid of something he didn't understand.

She looked up at me, tears in her eyes, "I'm so sorry Josh. She'd passed on before the paramedics even arrived."

Everything had stopped.

I felt nauseous. I felt so much pressure in my brain.

My ears were ringing.

I didn't understand.

"Passed on?" I questioned desperately, "you mean died?!"

I was afraid to hear the answer.

"Yes, mate." Dad's voice cracked.

I couldn't move.

I just need to stay perfectly still. If I didn't move, nothing would set in.

I don't know how long I sat there. At some point, dad grabbed my hand and held it. Mum hugged me tightly.

I couldn't concentrate. I couldn't think. What was I feeling? Angry? Sad?

Then I crumpled onto the table and realised I was crying.

Big, deep, heavy sobs I could feel in my chest.

None of us went back to sleep.

I wanted to go to the scene of the accident but my parents told me there was nothing to do there. But I just needed to know what happened. If there'd been a mistake. If she said anything... I just needed to know something.

My mind was stuck trying to comprehend Amber dying. She was talking to me just a few hours ago. We had plans for today. How will she be able to finish the bucket list if she's dead?

When my brain couldn't solve her death, it moved to anger. He'd done this. He'd done this to me. Worse than letting me jump into a toxic lake and nearly drown, Matt had taken the brightest light in my universe, my entire world, away from me.

———

A new sense of dread hit as the silence of the night gave way to the first bird songs of the morning, and the first glimpse of light chased off the darkness. It felt easy to hide in the cocoon that was the middle of the night, darkness felt small and safe, but daytime set life into motion, and I would never be ready for this day to move.

. . .

Andy texted me just after sunrise, telling me to call or come over anytime.

Then over the next hour, some of our group sent sympathy texts. Then angry, emotional messages from Amber's friends.

It was on the front page of the Courier Mail's website. A horrible photo of the car mashed into a pole. There it was, a road I'd driven a thousand times. A car I'd seen many times before. It was all so familiar that I couldn't connect it to the incident that shattered my life.

I studied the photo for a long time, looking for any sign that Amber wasn't in pain when it happened.

Any sign of Amber at all.

But there wasn't one.

Facebook was covered in tributes from all sorts of people at Amber's school. There were beautiful messages and photos from friends and classmates that showed off how she was always the life of the party.

In the mix were the very girls that Amber had leaned on my shoulder and cried about after they'd said horrible things to her. Maybe they were trying to right their wrongs. I just bitterly assumed they wanted to be part of the moment.

Initially I was scared to go online. I thought I'd see one thing about her and it would break me. But it didn't. Like the front page of the paper, it didn't feel like this was about Amber's death. It felt like eventually she'd wake up, message me and we'd laugh about some of the more corny tributes. I just wanted her here to roll her eyes at it all with me.

I put my phone down and lay on my bed.

I lay there with sticky eyes, my breathing shallow. Nothing felt fresh. I thought I should cry, but there was nothing inside me.

I lay there completely still.

Something in the back of my mind was working hard to find a solution, to fix this irreparable situation. This had to be all over soon, right? There had to be a weird mistake somewhere.

I clenched my fists, then my whole body, feeling so helpless and so frustrated. Yesterday Amber was here. Just a text message away. But today she wasn't.

And she never will be again.

How can that ever make sense?

Last night didn't feel weird, or significant. How can someone just disappear like that with no sign, any warning, any deep down gut feeling that things were wrapping up?

I must have laid on my bed for an hour, stuck in gross frustration. Numb to any sadness. Feeling so flat, no energy anywhere in or around me.

I picked up my phone again and texted Andy back.

JOSH: I just need to know what happened.

ANDY: Like why Matt was driving in the first place.... Or like the actual accident?

I sat upright in my bed. A new sick feeling weighing my stomach down deeper than any of the sadness had so far. I didn't want to acknowledge Andy's message. I didn't even want to look at it. I felt so vulnerable, so angry, so out of control, like my head was about to explode.

Matt wasn't licensed to drive. Matt was drunk. Matt's mum was coming to pick them up. That's what he'd said. Or is that what I'd assumed?

Either way, that means in Amber's most vulnerable moment, he took advantage of her and killed her.

That was murder, right?

17

Mum and Dad were sitting around the table playing cards when I stormed in demanding answers about why Matt could get away with murdering my girlfriend and nobody had even bothered to tell me about it. They looked up at each other, then asked me to come sit with them.

"You already knew?" I screamed, tears now flowing freely down my face.

"Yea mate, come and have a chat," dad replied with genuine pity.

"NO!" I screamed back at him. "You can't just tell me that this is something I'll understand one day or something like that. He's a murderer. I bet everyone is piling on the sympathy with him today because he was involved in something so horrible, but here's the truth: this is the kind of bullshit he does. This is the person he is. He needs to go to jail and they need to throw away the key."

"Josh," mum replied with a stern tone. "Nobody is saying anything like that. Now come and sit down so your father and I can tell you what we know."

I broke down in tears then. Dad rushed over to grab me before mum walked over and held us both. I cried deep sobs, letting out the frustration, the anger and the heartbreak.

Amber's parents had let mum and dad know Matt was arrested at the scene after telling police what happened. He didn't know Amber had died until they interviewed him early this morning. I didn't want to know how he responded, despite how much dad told me I should hear it.

Matt had his learner license and had taken his mum's car to the party. His parents were away for the weekend. He wanted to drive Amber home and leave me at the party. He'd been thinking about it all week.

It made me sick knowing that as I agonised over going to that party to try to rewrite the damage of what happened at the quarry when I was twelve, Matt was scheming a horrible plan ten times worse than what I was recovering from.

Days later the Courier Mail reported that Matt had confessed to intentionally giving Amber vodka when she asked for water. I called Andy and we put it all together. She'd been feeling sick after drinking too much and went to get water. She found Matt, someone she trusted, who fed her vodka, making her more sick. All so he could get her away from me.

As Andy said those words, "she found Matt, who she trusted," it was like the breath was knocked out of me. I couldn't speak. My mind filled with the image of Sammy telling me to go jump in the lake. It was the same scenario, but this time, the evil person succeeded in killing.

That night sleep came little. When it did I had the same nightmare; I was back in the lake, unable to find my way out of the water. Unable to breathe.

I'd wake up, sweating all over and breathing shallow, fast breaths.

Was that Amber's final seconds of life? Unable to find her way out of that car? Unable to breathe? Terrified and alone. Did she know she'd reached the end?

The thoughts would just keep circling in my head as I lay on my bed, feeling too scared to move. I was terrified new thoughts would come and I wouldn't be able to handle them. Then, suddenly, it'd all get too much, and I'd sit straight up, pulling my hair, wishing I could get the thoughts out of my brain.

I didn't understand how someone could just rip so many people's lives apart and the world would just go on as if nothing happened. How were people at the shops? Weren't they shocked and angry? How was school expected to just continue? How were memes being shared on Facebook like it was any other day?

How was no one else as pissed off as me?

Didn't we all just agree that Matt needed to be jailed for what he did?

He lied about helping someone when he was actually hurting them. He was trusted in that moment to help Amber and he did the worst possible thing to her. How could anyone call that a mistake or accident or whatever? He's a murderer.

———

The months that followed Amber's death were sometimes harder than the first few days. Some part of my brain, the part that comes up with ideas, would forget that Amber was gone. I'd be watching TV then suddenly get a rush of excitement. Perhaps tonight Amber and I could sneak out and go back up the mountain. Then, of course, in a heartbeat, reality would catch up and dread would fill my stomach. Sometimes it would knock the wind out of my lungs and I'd gasp in pain.

Amber's parents had given me the bucket list poster that Amber had put up above her bed. Now it was hung up above mine beside pictures of us and letters she'd written me during our time together. My Amber shrine.

A bucket list of dreams that could have changed the world, but would never be completed.

The nightmare that I was drowning still haunted my sleep and would lead me to waking up with a brain filled with what I believed Amber's final, horrifying moments were like.

I wished so badly that Andy, Cal and I left just minutes earlier and could have driven by as it happened and I could have saved Amber. Even if I couldn't have saved her, I could have been there to hold her and dream with her and tell her it was all going to be okay. She was the most wonderful person I'd ever met. How was it fair that she could die terrified and alone?

At school, I didn't want to deal with the sympathy or the questions. I told the boys pretty early on that I didn't want to talk about it, and if it came up, we shouldn't be weird about it. I hated walking into groups of people chatting who suddenly fell silent when I arrived, knowing full well they'd been talking about what happened and didn't know how I'd respond.

I felt so much anger. People seemed to think that I was hoping to get over the anger. I wasn't. I felt like everyone should be feeling this anger. For anyone who knew what happened, especially anyone who knew what Matt was like, there should be no other emotion they could feel but anger.

If I spent over 20 seconds thinking about Amber, it would really quickly spiral to me thinking about how I wish I could just go for a walk with her this afternoon, or sneak out late one night to the quarry with her. Then I wound up thinking about how Matt took that away.

I hated that people called it an accident. I get he didn't intend to kill Amber, or even to crash. But he took stupid risks to get what he wanted. His selfishness did it, even if he didn't mean to.

The more I thought about it, the more my whole body felt like it was about to explode. My brain was demanding we fix this. The anger made my stomach feel heavy and sick. My fists clenched like they needed to break down a door.

Having any conversation about Matt instantly brought on this anger. I'd yell and start accusing my friends of supporting him and I'd embarrass myself and then spend the next week having to fly under the radar to avoid the looks of people judging me.

So I avoided anything about Matt. I avoided conversations about him. I avoided social situations where he could be, or more generally, anyone who might mention him could be. I even avoided social media in case I came across anything to do with him.

And all that worked for nearly four months. Then Matt returned to school.

NOVEMBER 2012

18

MATT WAS GIVEN bail after his arrest, but he didn't come to school, or really even leave his house, until after his court date. I'm sure people at school spoke to him in that time, but I worked to pretend he just didn't exist.

When the court finally made their decision, the news filtered through school within minutes. We were silently working through a page of our textbook in maths when some boys at the back of the room started chattering.

"Uhm, boys, what's so important that you've decided you're above the rules?" Ms. Millie asked from her desk at the front of the room.

"Matt's court is done, miss," Michael Caspen replied. "Good behaviour, no conviction."

Most of the class reacted. A few sounded relieved for him, others sounded shocked.

"Oh, okay," Ms. Millie replied, looking unsure about what to do next. Suddenly her eyes darted across the room to me. She'd remembered this was going to be a big deal for me, but like everyone else around me when Amber's death came up she did not know how to act. I'd already closed my books and begun getting up.

"I'm just going to the bathroom," I said and walked out.

I sat in a toilet cubicle for the final two periods of the day. Friends messaged me their disgust at Matt getting away with murdering Amber. I told them I was doing fine, but actually, I was destroying every pen I had in my pencil case, digging them deeply into the wooden wall of the cubicle as I sat there silently crying, begging for the giant ball of pain in my stomach to go away.

I'd been certain that justice would be served for Amber. I was sure that the judge and jury would be disgusted by what Matt had done and they'd send him to jail for a long time. Instead, they decided Matt got to live his life as if nothing had happened.

I couldn't work out what happened next. Do we continue life as if Amber was never here? Do we pretend the cruel, painful few months just gone are now over and life goes back to normal? Do we have to pretend that Matt was innocent?

I couldn't do that. I couldn't do any of those things, but certainly not pretend Matt was innocent.

Every part of my body was tense. Seething with anger that Amber didn't get to live the awesome life that was ahead of her, and that Matt could just walk away, smug, like he'd done nothing wrong.

He's a murderer, and I'll never stop hating him for destroying the brightest light in my life.

Matt returned to school the day after his court case.

Some of my mates told him I didn't want his apology, I didn't want his sympathetic smile in the hallway, I didn't want to pretend we didn't know each other as we sat in class desks apart, I just wanted it to be like he didn't exist.

My friends, my family and even the school counsellor believed that this was my way of coping. I wouldn't be in conversations with Matt, wouldn't talk about him, wouldn't even look at him. It meant there was no awkwardness, no confrontation, and I wasn't angry or withdrawn all the time.

But deep down, Matt was all I thought about. I knew where he was throughout each day of school. I knew he'd been allowed to join the basketball team and played with them on weekends. I knew his four closest friends, all who'd supported him from the moment he killed Amber and had acted like he also was a victim of the accident.

Matt deserved none of it, and I wasn't going to pretend this outcome was okay. I would not give up on Amber like everyone else seemed to be.

Every night I'd go to bed filled with rage over another day that Matt got to live like nothing ever happened, and hoping for the day I'd get to remind everyone of who he really is.

———

Matt and I shared only one class, Mr Smith's religion class. I'd never considered that this would be the place where my perfectly worn mask would be ripped off, but then, one day in November the topic moved to the theme of forgiveness.

"The Bible teaches a very unanimous form of forgiveness," Mr. Smith began, sitting on his desk as he talked. "It proposes the idea that we should always seek to forgive any transgression, no matter the cost."

"In fact, Jesus himself proposes an unlimited amount of forgiveness for any person, despite their ongoing failures. The root of this forgiveness is the idea that we all do the wrong thing, so in order for us to be forgiven, we must also exercise that forgiveness."

I could feel myself going hot, like every eye in the classroom, especially Matt's, was on me. I knew I was the only person making the connection to this theme and what was happening with me and Matt. I'd been exemplary, never once bad-mouthing him, or talking about him at all.

But a fire was beginning to burn inside me and I wasn't sure if I could keep this one to myself. Every time Mr Smith mentioned forgiveness, it felt like he was aiming his words straight at me, baiting me to respond with why I was obsessed with bringing Matt down.

"*Matt made a choice*," I scribbled in my notebook, covering the page with my hand. "It was absolutely unacceptable in every lens you look at it through — legal, moral, just being a good person."

"I can't see how Hitler could be forgiven by God," someone had put their hand up, making a case from the back of the classroom.

I could hear the blood pumping in my ears.

I took a deep breath in.

"Hitler probably killed millions, but worse than that, he made them suffer before killing them. How could your God, who loves all people, possibly forgive that?" They continued.

"Well, that's the system of grace the Bible proposes in the New Testament," Mr Smith replied. "The idea that no matter what we've done, what our past is, that we can drop it all, turn around and start again... in fact, that is the story of one of the most prolific Bible writers, St. Paul. He murdered people who followed Jesus, the first Christians, and in an instant God revealed himself to Paul and then turned his power into good."

. . .

Over the past few months I'd learnt to subtly grit my teeth or clench my fists to suppress any sudden onset of wanting to scream at everyone about how messed up it was that Matt just got to live life as if he didn't murder Amber. I would not spoil my credibility. I needed it to call Matt out at the right time.

Then, there in that religion class, it all fell apart. I felt the rage rise from my stomach to my face, numbing every part of me as it went.

"But Hitler and Paul thought they were doing the right thing," I suddenly said, interrupting Mr. Smith. Everyone looked at me.

"Go on..." Mr. Smith said with a smile of optimism that the class conversation would get deeper than usual.

"Well, Hitler thought he was doing a great thing for the world. It doesn't matter how wrong he was, in his mind he was blessing the world and doing it a service.

"Paul thought Jesus and his followers were out to destroy everything great in his civilisation or something like that, right? The point is, they believed their hearts were in the right place, and that's how you can forgive something like that. That's not what I'd call unforgivable."

"Ahuh! So the heart of a man and his intentions can make things complicated!" Mr. Smith said, moving the conversation in the new direction he thought I'd proposed, before I interrupted again, a surge of adrenalin pushing through my veins.

"I think God would want us to side with the victim when it comes to forgiving people who are just selfish. You know, people who have stolen so much away from people just because it gives them some sick pleasure at that moment. I don't think God wants us justifying people's selfishness."

The moment felt surreal and out of body - as if I had no control of the words coming out of my mouth. I knew my tone was venomous and pointed. No one in that classroom would mistake what I was saying.

"It was an accident Josh. Do you think I would have seriously crashed that car on purpose?" Matt yelled from the back of the room. I could hear the pain in his cracking voice, but adrenalin surged in me again and I turned to face him. The first time I'd looked at him since he killed Amber.

"Oh, sorry Matt, are you feeling guilty about something?" I said sarcastically. I could see every person in the room looking at me. Shocked surprise written on each face.

"Okay boys, let's park this..." Mr. Smith tried to stop the horror that was unfolding in his classroom.

"Because you should be, because excuses like that only really work for people who's whole school life isn't a story of tripping over new kids at school, or trying to convince girls their boyfriends are losers, or taking any opportunity to humiliate people." I turned back to Mr. Smith. "Forgiveness is great, but it's for people who make mistakes, not for people who clearly get pleasure out of hurting others. Those people just stuff up the world for the rest of us. And I won't pretend that Amber's life was disposable by giving Matt Coulson that feeling that it's all in the past and forgotten," I said, pure hatred in my voice. Then I grabbed my books and walked out of the room.

Everything had become a blur. There was ringing in my ears. I needed to go somewhere, anywhere that wasn't near people. I felt like I was going to vomit, collapse and cry all at the same moment.

19

ABOUT 45 MINUTES after my outburst, Mr. Smith found me
sitting on a freshly painted park bench in the memorial
garden dedicated to the school's first principal. It was a
small space surrounded almost completely by hedges
ensuring maximum privacy. I'd been staring at the old
Italian style fountain in the middle of the garden for at least
half an hour.

I was numb, frozen, embarrassed, and so afraid of what
everyone was saying about me.

Then suddenly my entire body would tense and I'd feel
angry at Matt again. He was out there having lunch with his
friends, probably laughing at how stupid I'd looked, while I
was sitting here wishing a hole would swallow me up. How
does he keep getting away with being a terrible person?

"You know, Josh, CS Lewis wrote that forgiving does not
mean excusing. I think that's hard for us to grasp because
when someone commits a slight against us, we're certain
that an equal consequence, or more, must be served to
them. We feel a sense that justice must be served. But I
think if we're honest with ourselves, justice is not the main

reason we don't want to forgive. It's trying to work out what the hell to do with all this anger we feel."

I didn't want to hear this, it's like it was going in my ears, hitting a brick wall in my brain and then reverberating and causing even more anger.

Why was everyone so intent on forgiving Matt? He's a criminal. A murderer. And if he says he's sorry, he's not because this is who he has always been.

"Josh, you're doing a superb job of pretending you're the Josh before you lost a very special part of your life, but where does that go, son? Eventually, you'll have no real joy left to know how to put on that fake smile.

I'd like to believe people will see what this young lady brought into your life by who you've become.

What's the legacy of hers that will live on through you?"

He paused, sitting in silence for a few seconds.

"I'll be in my office until well after lessons today if you need to talk. Your classmates are worried about you. Make sure you make yourself known to them before the end of lunchtime."

He got up and walked away.

"Thanks," I mumbled. Not for the weird lesson. I still had no idea what he meant, and if anything I was a little angry that he was just another person trying to tell me I shouldn't be angry about something so messed up.

I was thankful that he had made me feel normal.

NOVEMBER 2020

20

"I DON'T THINK I've been this curious to review a restaurant in my career!" Lizzie said as we sat down at my restaurant's middle table. The large warehouse venue had six long tables running the length of its dining room, each with 130 chairs. The goal was to create a vibe of pulling up a chair at the community table, rather than everybody being off in their own little huddles.

During the lunchtime rush, it worked magically. I'm sure we'd introduced more than a few couples. On Friday and Saturday night, though, it felt more like a beer hall during Oktoberfest.

"I hope curious is a good thing and you aren't here to work out how such a terribly reviewed restaurant is still open," I replied with a lighthearted laugh.

I was excited too. We'd been waiting three months for the Courier Mail to send a reporter to profile *Amber's*. Finally, I was getting a chance to tell the story of why we exist.

"Oh, don't give me that! Everyone knows how good the food and beer are, Josh, but I want to understand the decor, and the name - there's a rumour in hospitality circles that it came out of a session with a psychologist?"

Beth, our floor service manager, brought over a big tasting platter of our signature menu items, giving me a wink and smile as she heard Lizzie mention the psychologist. Jarred, our bar manager, followed closely behind with two beer tasting paddles, each one carrying six small glasses of the beers we brewed on site.

"Well, are we on the record?" I gave Beth a cheeky grin.

"We certainly are," she laughed. "I'm hoping you aren't about to tell me it's a front for a crime family or something... I mean, a restaurant at Howard Smith Wharves could be tangled up in many things!"

She wasn't wrong. We sat in a warehouse underneath the Story Bridge. Today, we were surrounded by classy restaurants and a luxury hotel, all taking advantage of the views of the Brisbane River in front of us and towering city buildings to the right.

But just a few years ago, before all these old warehouses were done up to be the city's latest hotspot, they were old naval stores preserved by heritage listings, but falling apart as each storm, flood and scorching hot summer hit the city. It certainly wasn't the kind of area you would have walked into at night before the rejuvenation.

"It's more than just the name, the whole restaurant and brewery comes from that appointment," I picked up a crispy chicken Bao bun from the tasting platter, biting into it as Lizzie sipped a beer.

"When I turned 21, my parents gave me access to an inheritance left by my great grandfather before I was even born. He owned men's fashion stores and made a fortune from them, left a bit of money to everyone, but us great grandkids ended up with the lion's share. He'd left a note encouraging us to not just spend it, not just enjoy it, but use it to create our future. I'd intended to buy a house or something when the time was right."

"That must have been a pretty incredible discovery!" Lizzie said, trying to cover her mouth as she chewed through a halloumi slider.

"It was! I was sitting down to play board games with my parents when they told me they had something important to share. I thought one of them was dying to be honest."

I sipped a beer, a summer light brew, perfect for a day as warm as this one. It would only be a few more weeks before we'd need the air-con on in here, but for now, the air flowing from the large doors opened toward the river was doing enough.

"My teen years were a bit of a mess, to be honest. I went from having a pretty naive childhood to suddenly being involved in some stuff that messed me up a bit," I continued.

"The first few years after school, I was trying to make my mark in hospitality and I realised how angry I was at alcohol and party culture. Working in fancy restaurants and getting triggered by people drinking wasn't going down well. I ended up having to take some time off and just work in a supermarket."

Lizzie nodded at me, smiling sympathetically, still trying to catch up with the sudden emotional turn her interview had taken.

"My psychologist helped me realise that the anger towards alcohol stemmed back to another incident years before where my cousin had put me in a rough situation at a party and I'd never processed it all and moved forward. So there I was, just inherited a serious amount of money with a note to use it on setting up my future and my psychologist says 'You need to forgive your cousin and forgive alcohol, otherwise you're going to destroy your future.' I was shocked. It felt too obvious to be a coincidence, so I took it as a sign. Over the next couple of days, this place all came together in my brain."

"So, I can only imagine that the decor on the walls is matched with this story?" Lizzie looked around the restaurant as she said this.

The old wooden warehouse walls towering 20 feet up to the roof had been painted yellow. On the right wall was a giant picture of Sammy and I taken just after I signed the lease on this place and wrote her a letter of forgiveness and apology.

"So that's my cousin Sammy. When we were kids we were inseparable. I looked up to her like nothing else. What I didn't know is that my admiration meant a lot more to her than she'd ever let on. When we were far too young, she took me to a party and, long story short, nearly got me killed. Then asked me to lie about what happened and cover for her. That put our relationship on ice, and I didn't realise it, but the whole situation made me scared of everything. I jumped at my shadow."

"Ahuh, so the photo would suggest you've forgiven her then?" Lizzie had a questioning smile on her face.

"Forgiven her, and started a brewery to remind myself that other people's bad decisions shouldn't lead to me being too afraid to live - or drink beer!" I replied, lifting my glass in a cheers motion. Lizzie followed and clinked my glass.

"And the quote, well that's obvious," I continued after a sip, Lizzie turned around and snapped a picture on her phone of the huge words written in a stencil font next to the photo, "To forgive is to set a prisoner free and discover that the prisoner was you."

I looked out the giant open doors. The Brisbane River glistened as the mid-morning activewear crowd strolled by in groups along the boardwalk between the restaurant and the water.

"So, what's with the number 31?" Lizzie asked as she put her phone away, her attention now on the giant number painted on the left wall.

"So, the values we stand on are another key part of who we are. When I was 16, my girlfriend at the time snuck up to Whites Hill late one night in the school holidays. We talked about the White family that once had a home up there and how it became a bit of a drop in home. They had one of the most spectacular properties in the city at the time, and people were welcome to come over at any time, for any reason and just be welcome."

"We had a bucket list of dreams and the idea of having a home like the White's one day was bucket list item 31. The last item. This is that place. I don't care if you're here for a beer, something to eat, or just somewhere to sit without buying anything. This is a place to come and just be. To look at the river, the bridge, listen to some music, meet some old friends, make some new ones."

"Josh, I really thought I was coming out to the city's new up and coming trendy spot, but this place is going to end up writing itself into a beautiful feature article." Lizzie had a chuckle as she said this.

"I hope so," I said with a wink.

"So, is this high school girlfriend the rumoured secret business partner that no one knows about?" Lizzie brightly asked. Internally I cringed, knowing how guilty she was inevitably going to feel about asking this question.

"In some ways, yeah," I replied, trying to soften the blow, but Lizzie looked at me with a confused head tilt.

"She died in a car accident not long after," I finally replied. Lizzie's face dropped, she went to apologise. "No, no you weren't to know, but I didn't want anyone else owning this place with me, it's just our thing. Our little place."

"Oh Josh..." Lizzie was genuine in her sympathy and clearly lost for words.

"Amber was her name, by the way... naming this place *Amber's* had nothing to do with the colour of beer," I said with a cheeky smile.

"Just another surprise..." Lizzie tried to relax with a forced smile.

Not so long ago I would have taken a dig at Matt at this point. I would have found a way to say that a jealous, angry psychopath who showed no remorse caused the car crash. But I didn't need to do that now. His life was irrelevant to me. I was moving forward.

———

"It was great to meet you." Lizzie hugged me after I walked her back to her car after the interview.

"Yea, thanks heaps for setting this all up. It's really exciting to tell the story of what we're doing here."

"Well, I'm sure we'll run into each other at another happening venue sometime soon? I'd love to have a wine when we're both off the clock..."

"Not sure about that," I laughed, "I'm focused on *Amber's*. If I'm not here I'm safely at home dreaming up new ideas for this place."

"Oh," she paused, looking past me to the river. "Well, it was lovely to meet you."

NOVEMBER 2022

21

IT WAS warm out next to the road. A classic Brisbane summer night where the temperature won't drop to a comfortable level and anyone living without air-conditioning has no chance of sleeping. I'd just walked up the steep hill between the lobby of my building and the road leading onto the bridge and I was still catching my breath, sweat trickling down my face.

Cars zoomed past, and I felt guilty for hoping he wouldn't be on the bridge when I arrived. I didn't want him dead. Hopefully, he just decided to walk home.

But, as the footpath rounded onto the bridge, I saw him there, leaning over the edge, looking straight down. I paused, took a deep breath, and leant against one of the giant steel beams that stood between the footpath and the road. It was cool against my back. I questioned if I should do this. If I could have this conversation and not make things worse.

He didn't acknowledge me walking towards him and only looked over at me when he heard my footsteps come to a stop. His eyes locked with mine and I saw a mix of confusion that quickly gave way to fear, almost like a cowering child afraid of punishment.

"Hello Matt," I said, hoping to sound warm.

"Oh, great." Matt sounded defeated and threw his head back to stop more tears from coming. His eyes were bloodshot.

"So, how's things?" It seemed like an obvious place to start.

"I can't have you bring it all up mate," his voice was strained and although he was talking a bit louder to compensate for the traffic rushing by on the bridge, his voice gave away that he was on the edge, fighting for his last ounce of respect. "I don't need to hear how much I messed you up."

I stood and stared at him. A quick flash of anger hit me. He didn't just mess me up, he took away Amber's life. She'd be overseas now, saving young girls, but she's dead. Because of him. He didn't get to just say that was too hard for him to deal with.

Memories of Amber came rushing to my mind. In our final 18 months together at school, he'd managed to get his life back to normal. He got to go to year 12 Formal. He got to put preferences in for university and plan what he'd do with the rest of his life. He got to graduate. He got to go to schoolies. His life got to go on as if he didn't set Amber up to be sitting in the passenger seat of the car he smashed into a pole leaving her to die terrified and alone.

Ten years later, though, he clung to a bridge railing like he was at risk of being swallowed by the earth. His tear soaked, bloodshot eyes were staring at me like I was in control of his fate.

. . .

A truck zoomed over the bridge, tearing me back to reality with an ear piercing rumble and furious blast of air. Instantly, I realised my role here. I had more power than anybody else to help Matt decide where his story went next. If I walked away, said nothing, even reminded him what he did to Amber, I wouldn't get in trouble, not legally at least, but who am I after that?

Someone's life hung in the balance in front of me.

"No need for any of that," I finally replied, forcing a small smile to appear, "I live just up there, come and grab a beer."

I reached out for Matt's hand, just to pull him away from that railing. The moment his hand hit mine though, I felt my lungs release, like I'd let out a breath I'd be holding for longer than I could remember.

———

I clinked down two bottles of our cider on my outdoor table as Matt sat there quietly staring down at the spot he'd just been on the bridge.

"I'm really sorry," he abruptly said when I sat down. "I hate who I was in high school. But Amber didn't get put off by me being an asshole sometimes. She'd tell me off and just keep talking to me and not be all pissy with me."

This made me smile with memories of Amber. One of her many wonderful qualities was her ability to let go of small grudges fast.

"When I saw you guys together, it was just so weird. I was sure you'd convince her to drop her friendship with me. You know, like some kind of ultimatum, and I couldn't handle the pain of her choosing you."

He turned his gaze to me. "I'm really sorry, Josh. The night of the party, I just wanted to do something so that you'd see she was also my friend. To make sure you knew that she'd pick me sometimes."

I sat there slowly nodding, trying to process his words. Silence hung between us again.

"For ten years I haven't been able to forget the last conversation we had before the party," Matt eventually continued. "I told her I was sick of everyone at school and I didn't even know why and she said I should stop trying to convince everyone I was better than them. I thought it was stupid, but deep down, I know it was true. I was embarrassed she'd seen right through me."

A million thoughts were running through my mind, but I couldn't catch any of them. Tears were welling in my eyes as sadness built inside me, not a fresh sadness from tonight's events, but a deep sadness that had felt like it had been waiting to be noticed.

Time passed in silence. At least a minute or two had gone. A siren had wailed across the bridge and long since disappeared into the dull roar of the weekend night.

"Thanks for apologising," I finally said, and I meant it.

We stared at the bridge. Cars zoomed along, some loud, some quiet.

"I think I'm ready to forgive you, Matt."

"I don't know what that means if I'm honest, but I know I don't want to live with this anger anymore."

I leant back in my chair and exhaled. Matt's head was in his hands and I could see him slowly sobbing. I wasn't sure if I was making things better or worse for his mental state.

"I mean, I'm sure I'll feel anger toward you from time to time, but I want that anger to be my problem, not your problem. It's time to get off this moral high ground I got on when I was 16."

"Thank you," he replied in a cracked, honest voice.

"And that anger, that horrible thing I spewed at you in

class all those years ago, the way I treated you like you weren't even worthy to be looked at by me for the rest of our time at school, I have to tell you mate, that wasn't just about you. I had some stuff... some stuff from my childhood that I'd just started really dealing with."

"And I was so mad at Amber. I'd tried so hard to talk her out of going to that party, but in the end, she convinced me it was just going to be good fun. After it all happened, I was so desperate to tell her I was right and she was wrong. I was so mad at her for making us go that night."

"I read the article about you in the paper a couple of years ago." Matt looked up at me. "Sorry for making all those memories come back..."

"Nah, don't be," I brushed him off. "You either do something with the pain or it'll own you. I thought those horrible experiences had stopped owning me when we opened the brewery, but it wasn't till I was walking down to that bridge tonight that I realised how pissed off I was at you...at Amber...even at Andy for begging me to be at that party! I've just been putting on a mask, pretending I'm over it. But I was still pissed off. Still holding it against people. Still not letting myself give 100% trust to anyone."

Saying it out loud, I realised that Amber's not having a co-owner wasn't because I wanted it to just be me and her, but because I refused to trust anyone enough to run a business with me. Andy had wanted to be an investor. He came offering cash and exciting dreams of us running a venue together, and I'd turned him down repeatedly.

"I probably read that article ten times over, thinking somehow you'd managed to forget about me and what I did. I was obsessed with wanting you not to hate me anymore. I almost came into your bar a few times just to see if you'd even acknowledge me."

· · ·

Matt shared with me about the last ten years of his life. He lost friends and some family within months of the crash. People gave up on him, just like I had.

In the years that followed, he became so emotionally crippled from overthinking every social interaction he had. He always believed he'd said something that offended, upset, or hurt everyone, and so he just stopped interacting with people.

I'd spent the last ten years angry, looking at the world, believing most people didn't care who they hurt, as long as they got their way. Matt had spent those same years needing me to learn that wasn't true.

He stayed at my place that night, then in the morning went and saw a doctor.

———

The next night I drove out to Andy's place and made him wander into the bushland with me, a cooler bag between us holding a couple of beers and a packet of scotch fingers.

He told me about his date last night as he followed me through the bush and up the mountain. Cicadas sung as the pale moonlight poked through the trees and guided our way up the path. It had been ten years since I was last on that track, yet it felt so familiar.

When we finally reached the clearing, it was like a single day hadn't passed since I was last there. The grass was cut as always, the dark quarry filled the space beneath us, and the suburbs of Brisbane were laid out ahead of us.

We sat down and cracked a beer, then a scotch finger.

"Weird to be back?" Andy asked.

"Yea," I said, staring at the millions of stars in the sky,

forever a reminder of the wonderful secrets Amber and I shared under them, "but I think I'm ready to move back out here."

"Finally going to leave that bridge?" He asked, smirking at me and raising his beer toward the Story Bridge off in the distance.

I took a deep breath, smiled, my face still looking toward the sky.

"I've wanted to tell her 'I told you so' since the day it happened." I was trying hard not to cry, but my voice was betraying me and Andy put his hand on my shoulder. "I wanted to tell her I was right, that we never should have gone to that damn party."

"I've been waiting to tell her."

There I was, in almost the same spot as the time ten years ago when Amber looked deeper into my soul than anyone ever had and told me things about myself I'd never realised before.

"One night we sat here, Amber and I, and she took me on about how much I was missing out on stuff I'd love because of that silly thing that happened down at the quarry. She was so right, but of course the next thing that happened was... well... the accident," I stopped, taking stock of my thoughts.

"Amber died, and it's the worst thing that's ever happened to me, but it was ten years ago and it feels like I haven't lived a day since."

"I mean, you own one of the most popular restaurants in the city..."

"Sure. I've done things. I've made sure I saw the psychologists, wrote the forgiveness letter, said the right words. I did the things to make sure that people didn't think of me as some charity case. But I can't keep denying that I'm still the traumatised and angry year eleven kid

147

doing things just to create the impression that I'm doing fine."

"Who'd have thought it was Matt that made me realise I've been knocked flat on my back, too scared to move for a decade?"

"He might have been the only person that could have made you realise..." Andy replied with a smile. "You're right, hey, most days I encounter another middle-aged person who has spent their whole life ignoring trauma from their teenage years that they're now vomiting all over the people in their everyday life in the form of being horrible and manipulative."

We both looked up at the stars.

"I need to piss," Andy quickly jumped up and walked back over to the bushes behind us, dried leaves cracking under his feet as he got there.

I pulled out my phone, opening the photo I'd taken at my parents house before Andy arrived. Our bucket list, on paper faded and worn after hanging on a wall for ten years, shone up at me from the screen.

I didn't need to tick these items off. If anything I needed to stop ticking off items to get done. But I did need to live the spirit of the bucket list. To have dreams and to chase them. To be excited for life and unafraid to live it.

I looked back up at the stars, then whispered,

"Sorry it took so long, Amber."

DID YOU ENJOY THIS BOOK?

Thank you so much for reading *Our Dreams Were Waking Up*, I had such a great time getting to know Josh and Amber and I hope you did too.

If you enjoyed reading I'd love it if you could post a short review on Amazon or Goodreads . Even a simple line like "I enjoyed this book" can be really helpful! Your feedback helps the book become more visible to other readers, giving me the chance to write more!

JOIN MY READER CLUB!

I'd love to share some little short stories, news about my next novel and of course give you early access to my upcoming books, if you want to be part of it sign up to my newsletter by visiting scottymcdonald.com.au or scanning this QR code

ABOUT THE AUTHOR

Scotty McDonald lives in Brisbane, Queensland, Australia with his beautiful wife and their sweeter than chocolate baby girl. Scotty has worked in radio and television since before he finished high school, but his secret love for late night adventures with friends and beautiful stories about falling in love has left him with a head full of book ideas.

If you'd like to be the first to know about what he writes next make sure you join his Reader Club by heading to my website, https://scottymcdonald.com.au or by scanning this QR code

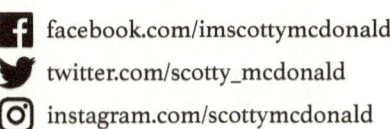

facebook.com/imscottymcdonald
twitter.com/scotty_mcdonald
instagram.com/scottymcdonald